By the same

Proxima West

Starchaser

Hot Knife

Blowback

Speedbomb

Amy and the Fox

Before the Gulf

John Lake

Published by Armley Press, Ltd, 2022
ISBN 978-1-9160165-5-2
© John Lake

Typesetting: Ian Dobson
Cover design: Mick Lake
Production: Mick McCann
Printed by Lightning Source

To friends I made in Koh Samui, Tioman, Bali… and Helsinki

Part One

Gulf of Thailand

Before the Gulf

One

Start with one true sentence, said Ernest Hemingway, and make it the truest sentence you know.

This is the great novelist's advice for kicking away writer's block and beginning a story. Unfortunately, as set down here, they're only *words to that effect*, my hazy memory's best effort at reported speech, which is why I don't put anything in quotation marks. The exact truth of them is impossible to confirm or deny without a smartphone or wi-fi – things I left behind long ago in a different place, a former life.

All I possess here is a pay-as-you-go Motorola, bought with the last of my cash dollars from a street market that I passed through in KL on my long journey to where I am now. It makes calls and sends texts and that's it. Not even a camera. In fact, I don't own any camera at all and I don't normally let anybody take my picture. That phone, which I carry with me but rarely use, and a plain Timex battery-operated wristwatch that gives you the time and date and nothing else, are my only day-to-day connections to the world of mediated information.

So I stop writing after that first sentence and lay the pen down on my notebook on the bar top and use my knuckle to scrape a seam of sweat from my upper lip, then wipe the back of my hand across my forehead; it comes away dewy wet.

The lone sentence crosses the page less like the opening of a book and more like a maxim captured and noted for future reference; an idea hunted down and locked in a cage. But is it true or not? The sense is authentic but is it true to Hemingway's standards? And if it isn't, is that going to make me a bad writer?

'Another beer, Danny?' I say, lifting the empty bottle in front of me and waving it at the bartender, who is perched on a stool in the far corner of his domain doing something with an iPhone. 'Danny' was how this young guy, the only person I've ever seen tending bar here, introduced himself the first time I came. His real name, I found out later, was something I couldn't pronounce at the time and have forgotten since. A lot of people on the island give themselves western nicknames to make it easy for the tourists, especially if they're involved in that particular racket – and everybody here is, whether they know it or not.

Danny pulls a fresh bottle of Singha from the fridge, pops the cap and stands it in front of where I'm sitting on a high bar stool with my elbows on the counter. He knows not to bother wasting a frosted glass on me. Then he scribbles a new bill, tears it off the pad and places it on top of my previous bill. I nod and smile at him.

'Thanks, Danny.'

'No problem, Mike.'

I told Danny on a whim, when we first met, that my name was Mike Hammer, and I've still never corrected it, with him or anyone else. Incredibly, in all my time here, not once has anyone raised the subject of the detective of the same unlikely name created by Mickey Spillane. Maybe his books never made it this far east. Danny is a friendly, helpful kid who I happen to trust, and one day I should do him the courtesy of putting things right. But not today nor probably any other day soon.

He turns away to serve a customer waiting on the beachfront side of the hut, a deeply tanned German guy with a tattooed body and a baseball cap on a shaved head, and I turn to my second afternoon beer. Two is an acceptable number for me before I have to go to work. Two I can handle without any loss of the physical or mental functions needed for my job.

Getting back to writerly thoughts, I look at the bottle of beer, study the design of the lion on the label and try to see it afresh after seeing it a thousand times before. I observe the droplets cutting tracks through condensation as they trickle down the cold glass. Over my shoulder to my right I can hear the voices of beachgoers and the sound of surf, the sea not thirty metres away. I can smell it. I think carefully about how I could write it down in words that are true to what I am doing and what is happening around me.

The day has brought plenty of sunshine and I have enough money to pay for my beer, and I can live as I choose. The world feels like a beautiful place to be in, and I try to pin the moment down accurately in my mind. But are these true sentences? Because, for me to be a good writer, I believe that my sentences have to be true in the way Hemingway meant it when he said what he said.

Did he *say* it, or did he *write* it?

I swallow a mouthful of beer from the neck of the freshly opened bottle. The cold fizz in my throat and the iciness of the glass bottle in my hand are gorgeous to experience in all this heat. Then, the first little breeze of the day comes off the sea as the long hot afternoon prepares to dip swiftly towards a warm night.

I put the bottle down and pick up my pen and look at that one true, or possibly not quite true, sentence and think about other sentences that might follow it and what they might be about. They could be about whether 'quite true' and 'not quite true' are at all possible, whether there can ever be fractions or gradations of truth…

Thinking that, I realise I have fallen into a trap. Does it matter what the sentences are about? Doesn't it only matter that they are true? Can they, in fact, *be* true sentences if they are merely *about* something? 'Don't write *about* it, just *write* it,' I can hear Hemingway growling in my head. He probably never actually said that. Or maybe he did.

I am so far away from the truth in my thoughts now that I put the pen down again and close my notebook. That's enough writing for today. When I think of something true, I'll write some more of it, whatever it is that I'm writing.

I'm coming to the end of that second beer when I hear Lily shouting at me from down the path that skirts the bar to the main road.

'Hey! You! Got job!'

Lily is the only person in town who does know my real name, though she has never used it and never would. She just calls me 'Hey You'. Her unmistakable squawk always registers when I hear it – as familiar as Mum's voice calling me from down the lane when I was a kid, but more welcome than my mother's voice to my adult ears. I see Danny give me a look and a grin. He heard Lily too. The whole beach heard her. I square up with the kid and we do a hand clasp and I throw my stuff into my satchel then head via the path to the main road out front.

Two

It's nearly twilight now and the street is busy with traffic and tourists, and all the lights are coming on and the insects are coming out. I look up and see the first fruit bat of the evening lolloping across a velvety blue sky.

'Here, here, lady for you.'

Lily is impatient with my wildlife spotting and is pulling me by my arm towards a woman waiting by my propped-up scooter who is looking up and down at the bustling street activity and dodging gutter-hugging mopeds as they buzz close by. The calm and quiet of the beach might as well be fifty miles away instead of just fifty metres.

The woman looks somewhere in her thirties, wears strap-around sandals and a sleeveless flower-print dress. Her arms, neck and shoulders show a mild tan and a natural paleness underneath the dress line. An Alice band pushes back long dark hair from a blue-eyed, clear-skinned, stoically smiling face. A small backpack hangs off one shoulder and on the narrow pavement next to her stands a mid-sized slate-grey suitcase, one of those with wheels and a retractable yoke.

'Hi, you looking for a lift?' I say to get her attention.

'Oh! You're English, aren't you?' she says. My manner rather than my accent or my looks is what gives it away.

'Is that a problem?' I try not to make it sound like a threat, keeping my intonation friendly.

'No. Of course not. I'm just surprised. Cycle taxis are always locals.'

I give her my gentlest smile. 'Then I guess I'm the exception that proves the rule.'

It's a corny thing to say but I don't want to lose the fare. I ask her where she wants me to take her and she gives me the name of a swanky resort on the other side of the headland down the coast, some six or seven miles farther along the road.

"'Scuse my asking, but how did you end up here?'

'There was obviously some mix-up in communication with the taxi driver,' she tells me. 'He thought it was here I wanted to be and once I'd paid him and got out he took off before I realised I was in the wrong place.'

It sounds unlikely. I don't know a single driver who can't speak good English or who doesn't know the name and location of every hotel and resort on the island. Maybe he needed to knock off suddenly. But what would make him ditch a fair? Hunger, sleepiness, his favourite soap opera? I don't ever hear of those things interfering with the hustle for the almighty tourist dollar.

Still, I'm not here to argue with the woman. We agree on a price and I bungee-cord her case onto the back of the Honda Click. Lily is still hovering for her commission, and I slip her a note for her cut of the deal in advance of the agreed fare, which never escapes her ears even when the street is rowdy like this, or even at its rowdiest, at three o'clock in the morning.

I straddle the bike and kick the prop away before inviting the woman to climb on the back, where she sits snug between me and her case. I look back to check everything is secure.

'You ready?'

The woman clasps the sides of my waist at the place they call 'love handles' and we move out into the slow, wriggling stream of evening traffic.

Three

There is only one serviceable road south from where I picked up my passenger and it follows the coast around the headland rather than cutting across it because the east shore, all the way along, is where the trade is. The journey takes us through a string of erstwhile fishing villages, all joined up now in long strips of touristic development.

Sometimes we hit a lull, barely describable as rural, between these bright stretches of bars, shops, shacks and seaview hotels, and the road gets quiet enough for us to talk over the sound of the engine in the warm, darkening night air.

I'm not fussed about talking as a rule, but my passenger clearly is. I get the feeling she's talking to reassure herself that everything is normal and safe. She must know as well as everyone else that crimes against tourists are rare here because they're so severely punished. I don't tell her this explicitly but I make the effort to talk back if it will make her feel better. I make a point, another rule, of not asking any personal questions, such as where she's from. That makes tourists nervous if asked too soon, a common mistake made by many of my local competitors, costing them the opportunity of repeat jobs or long-term hire. Tourists, especially lone travellers, think that caginess will protect them, and local operators, coming from a culture of frankness and openness, fail to understand and respect this western need for privacy, often to their cost. Her accent could be Irish, I can't place it yet. When she asks what brought me to live out here on the other side of the world, I give her my usual story.

'I had some romantic notion that I could come here and be a writer. You know, write a book.'

'What kind of book?'

'The kind that sells.'

'And how did that work out?'

'Yeah, great. The chopper's gonna pick me up and fly me back to the yacht once I've dropped you off.'

After half an hour on the coast road and a short climb uphill we draw up to the gates of the resort, which are framed beneath an elaborate stone archway and flanked by two big flaming sconced torches that throw dancing shadows on the unevenly-surfaced whitewashed walls of the compound. Beyond the gates a sky-blue band of illuminated swimming pool, emerald bursts of shrubbery, and the nestling up-lights that mark the pathways through the grounds are all I can see from where we have stopped. Everything seems quiet, balmy, unpeopled. Though, when my hearing adjusts after cutting the bike engine, I catch distant voices and a smattering of laughter from somewhere behind the walls.

'This is it,' I say needlessly.

The woman, whose name has not featured in our chit-chat, climbs off the saddle and I prop up the bike and go to unstrap her case from the back. While I'm doing this, the woman is walking around, stretching her legs after the long bike ride. She rubs her bare arms against what passes for an evening chill in these parts, and finds herself drawn towards the heat radiating off the burning torches. I wait with her case by the bike while she strolls up to the gates for a better look inside. Her head turns, looking, then freezes at something or someone she sees inside the grounds that I can't see. She ducks out of somebody's sight behind the gatepost before trotting back to the bike on tiptoes.

'Shit, they're here already. I can't face them like this.' She seems to say this to herself, because it means nothing to me. 'Change of plan,' she says to me. 'I need to find somewhere else to stay. Can you take me back, please?'

'To the airport?'

'Back to the town.'

'For the same fare again, I can.' No commission to Lily this time.

'Fair enough.'

I re-tie the suitcase to the bike and don't ask any questions as she hops back onto the saddle. As long as I get paid, I can ride her around the island till the water buffalos come home.

Four

I ride her back into town to the only place I can reasonably take her, which is Lily's Beach Huts, not a hundred metres from where she first got on the bike, because Lily would kill me if she heard I'd taken a potential customer anywhere else. I park the bike in the garden of Lily's house and trundle the woman's suitcase along the path to reception, and the woman follows me under a bower of garden foliage and the noise of cicadas and the smell of flowers replacing petrol fumes.

Outside reception we find Lily sitting in a rattan chair, smoking a cigarette and gazing towards the sea, keeping watch over the ten beach huts that weave an uneven lane through her half-acre of land from here to the shoreline. She looks up, sees me, then the woman.

'Oh! You back!' She addresses me: 'You break down or something? You know no money back.' Lily is tenacious as a tiger once she has cash in her fist. The metaphor is faulty because a tiger can't make a fist, but I think the sentence makes its point.

'Relax,' I tell her. 'She needs a room for the night.'

'You not like Shiri Palace?' says Lily, namechecking the upmarket resort that we've just returned from.

'She needs a room for the night, Lily, all right? We got any free huts?'

'Free?'

'I mean vacant.'

'Last one,' says Lily. 'Up here near house, not beachside. Near to beach those hut go first. All full.'

'So the one next to mine,' I say, seeing as my hut has always been the one nearest the house. I turn to the woman. 'Is this all right? We could trawl round some of the classier places if you like but you've seen how mad it is out there, it could be a long and fruitless search. This place is cheap and

16

spartan but it's clean and it's got its own loo, a fan and a mosquito net with, I promise you, no holes in it.'

'Hey You, what you mean, "cheap"?' Lily butts in. 'Good price for you, madam.'

'No,' says the woman, 'this is fine.' I can see that she's trying to be cool with it. 'It's away from the road, it's quiet...' She's selling it to herself: the stridulating crickets, the sound of the waves kissing the shore not far away, just beyond the rustling palms and the swaying string hammocks...

'It's quiet now,' I tell her, 'but wait till the clubbers come back at four in the morning.'

'Don't worry, I've got earplugs.'

I don't tell her about the prostitutes that some of the men will bring back to the huts. I don't want to botch the deal, I want my finder's commission from Lily, and anyway she'll work it out for herself once the lager louts start up their whoopee-machines. I got used to the sex noises a long time ago. They don't bother me, or if they do I don't admit it to myself. Everyone minds their own business, there's rarely any trouble, and by morning the girls are gone. One time, I'm told, before my time, a tourist tried bringing a kid back for the night. Lily soon put a stop to it, sent the bloke packing and put the word around about him. That kind of thing happens plenty in certain cities on the mainland but the locals here won't put up with it on their island. The story goes that the man in question was later found dead, washed out to sea, but the police questioned no one about it. I suspect it is only a story. If so, it's a good one, honest and true.

The woman fossicks a purse from her backpack to pay Lily for one night upfront.

'You know,' I say, 'there's very little serious crime against tourists here but there is petty crime. You should get yourself a money belt because sneak thieves—'

'I know. I've got one. I just haven't transferred it yet. Okay?'

She's a little flustered. I shut up and let her pay. Lily gets up out of her chair and reaches into reception and hands me the last key off the rack and I pull a Maglite from my satchel and light the woman's way to her accommodation.

'You never asked me my name,' she says as we sidestep tree roots and fallen husks in the sandy topsoil by the light of the torch. 'You don't ask many questions, do you?'

'No.' I leave it a beat. 'I suppose, seeing as we're gonna be neighbours – '

'It's Laura.'

I glance back at her over the shoulder that's pulling her case. In the dark orchard, with the soft light from the veranda of Lily's house behind her, she's just a silhouette.

'Hi, Laura, pleased to meet you.'

'Don't I get to know yours?' she asks when I don't offer it.

I stop walking and turn around, pointing the torch beam down between us so as not to dazzle her with it. 'I'm sorry, I'm being rude. I'm – Mike.'

'Hi, Mike.'

We shake hands.

'This is you,' I say. 'Hut nine...' I direct the torchlight at the number scorched into the surface of a coconut shell cunningly nailed to the door we've reached. '... Without meaning to sound like a stalag camp guard.'

She laughs politely at my lame POW joke.

I step up onto the porch, put the key in the lock and push the door open, hefting the case through the doorway ahead of Laura, who follows me in. Inside the hut, the fug of intense warmth that has been mounting all day in there hits us both. A renewed wave of sweat sets my skin tingling.

'There is electricity,' I say, flicking the switch to light up the naked 25-watt bulb that hangs from the ceiling. 'Some places I've stayed in just give you an oil lamp.'

'Tell me about it,' she says.

The dingy light is enough to reveal the bed with its mosquito net suspended above it, the freshly laundered sheets and pillow, a bedside table, the electric fan, a mirror on the wall, the door to the toilet and *mandi* in the back washroom. The wooden floorboards are swept clean and are free of cockroaches. It's all stuff she can see for herself so I just stand there for a moment without saying anything, waiting for her to give me the okay to leave her to it.

'Thanks, Mike. It must seem a bit weird, my going all that way only to turn around and come back again.'

'Hey, it's none of my business.'

'No.' The way she says this and the way she casts her eyes down make me feel like I just told her it's not my problem. And she's right to take it that way because, whatever it is, it isn't.

'If you need food, well – ' I wave a hand back in the direction of the main strip. 'You know where it all is. Restaurants and snack bars stay open till eleven, or midnight, some of them. Bars, dance clubs, ladyboy cabarets, kickboxing, whatever turns you on… All human life is here, as someone famous once said.'

'It was Anthony Burgess. You should know that if you're going to be a writer.'

I smile. 'Hm. Anthony Burgess. The *Clockwork Orange* guy, right? Who'd have guessed?'

Laura reaches for her purse to offer me a tip.

'No, forget that. If you need ferrying anywhere tomorrow, knock on my door. Hut ten. If I'm not around, ask the landlady, she'll know where to find me.'

'O-kay. Are you going?'

'Yeah. It's still early, there are jobs waiting out there. My workday's barely begun.'

'Of course. Of course. Well, thanks for everything. And… have a good evening.'

'You too.'

She leaves the door open behind me and I hear her step out onto the veranda as I walk back through the orchard to where Lily is still sitting. Lily has lit a mosquito coil, and another cigarette. As I walk by, she hisses at me:

'Hey You! Why she come back here from Shiri Palace?'
'I don't know, Lily. I didn't ask, I just did the job.'
'You not interested to know?'
'I didn't say that, Lily. I just don't ask. Sometimes, that way,' I say, tapping the side of my nose meaningfully, 'you find out more.'
I'm feeding her bollocks, of course, but perhaps there's a little truth in it.

Five

The season is high and there are plenty of jobs for everybody on a night like this. Most of my runs in the early part of the evening are short hops between bars and clubs up and down the main strip, back and forth, back and forth, ferrying giddy young Aussies and Europeans who are happy to part with the price of a drink if it's for a ride that'll get them to the next drink quicker. If there's a group of them on the lash together, and they don't want to split up the gang, I'll team up with other riders and we'll take them in convoy. There are always riders to hand, touting along the strip, and you might be surprised at how often the spirit of co-operation is understood to trump the demon-god of competition.

Later, when the clubs start to empty, the longer, more profitable runs out along the coast will come, when all that a shagged-out raver desires is his or her distant hotel bed, and they will pay any affordable price to get to it.

On a coffee and snack break in a little flyblown bamboo roadside bar some time before midnight, I pick up a stray copy of the local newspaper and see something about an international conference happening this week on the island. My reading ability in the local language isn't great, and the item mentions a bunch of acronyms that mean nothing to me, something high-tech or academic, but before I turn the page the name of the conference venue catches my eye: Shiri Palace. The resort is said to be fully booked for the coming weekend with conference-goers.

It follows that if Laura has a reservation there then she must be here for the conference. I scan for her name among the handful of prestigious delegates that are listed in the newspaper article but there is no Laura. I snap the paper shut, drink my coffee and tell myself it's still none of my business.

Not long after midnight there's a lull in taxi business when all the sensible get-a-good-night's-sleep diners have eaten up and gone back to their hotel nightcaps and all the drinkers and ravers have rooted themselves to their chosen dance floors and insanity spots. For us, the loafing hour. I stand around idling by the bike, chatting and joking and killing the time with other guys working the strip.

When I first rocked up from nowhere with a shitty old Yamaha moped and started imitating what the locals were doing to make a living, plenty weren't happy about it. But I stuck it out and after a long time they learned to leave me alone and after another long time they learned to get on with me. It helped when I picked up some of the language, though it took me an age. But I was always okay. I had no beef with anyone who didn't have a beef with me first and I knew how to keep my nerve and take care of myself. I made it known that I wasn't going to go away unless it was to please me, not anyone else.

Now I don't get any trouble from the locals. I've been here five years and my face is known. 'That's Mike, he's okay,' they say. It helps that I look mixed race. I am mixed race, just none of it their race. And yes, sure, there are the bad 'uns, the bullies, the racketeers, the small-time overlords, but I generally keep my head down and let Lily deal with them, which she does through a combination of impish charm, iron will and respect for seniority. You don't snap at the higher-ups in the food chain, not unless you're fighting for your life.

I pick up the last job of the night around four a.m. outside the audaciously named Copland. At that hour, the side street leading away from this huge barn of a nightclub is choked with tired revellers. They shuffle and stumble and trip over one another like a footsore column of refugees on a long march, two thousand of them every night in high season, all drunk or drugged into a zombie-like state, and shell-shocked that the music has ended. Some of them are still wild and in a hurry to find the next bar but the impossibility of moving anywhere quickly soon knocks it out of them. Either way, it's rich pickings for cycle taxis.

A young western couple, boyfriend and girlfriend, travel buddies or whatever, spot my bike and wobble towards me holding hands so as not to lose each other in the shifting press of bodies. They give me the name of a hotel about fifteen minutes up the coast but I can't take both of them at once so I beckon a nearby mate, Guntur, over and he takes the boy and I take the girl and we do the run nose to tail. After we've dropped them off Guntur and I ride companionably back into town together and he goes off scouting for more jobs down by the clubs while I decide to call it a night.

I park the bike deep in, out of view from the street. Lily's house is quiet, all the lights are off. She'll be fast asleep at this hour. She'll be up and about in another two. I switch on the Maglite and head through the trees towards my hut and the sound of the ocean. Soft warm light glows in the windows of two or three huts and the sound of a girl moaning comes from one of them. I'm on my porch and about to unlock the door when another light, blue and cold, catches the corner of my eye. On the other side of a dark divide, Laura is sitting out on her veranda and the light is coming from the screen of her mobile phone.

'It's only me,' she whispers across. I walk over to her. 'Couldn't sleep. Reverse jet lag. Slept too much on the plane.'

'Oh yeah? Business class or first class?' No one sleeps well in economy.

'Pull up a pew.'

I grab the other wicker chair from its corner and lift it across making sure to create no loud noise. I sit down and tilt the chair back and rest my feet up on the porch rail.

'God,' says Laura, keeping her voice low, 'they've been at it for an hour.'

I laugh just a little, then a squeal and a grunt from hut seven makes us both laugh louder.

'He's getting his money's worth,' I say. 'Sorry to be crude about it.'

A small wooden table stands between our two chairs with an opened bottle of a reputable single-malt on it. The level hasn't sunk much below the neck.

'Nice,' I say, lifting and inspecting the bottle in the light from her cabin window and noticing the torn half of a duty-free strip stuck to the neck.

Laura is back to peering at her phone. 'Help yourself,' she says. 'No glasses, I'm afraid, but you can't catch anything from a bottle.'

'Except liver damage.'

I lift the whisky bottle to my lips and take a decent sip. It tastes like home, which I don't much like, and I put the bottle back down.

'I'm surprised you can get a signal,' I say, nodding at the phone.

'Then you'd better come out of the nineteen-nineties. Sorry, I'm being rude, now.' She thumbs a button and the screen goes dark and she turns towards me. 'Did you have a good night? Make some money?'

'I did all right.'

'No more long pointless trips to the Shiri Palace?'

She seems determined to tell me it – her story. She keeps dangling it in front of me. And although I'm not ready to bite, I seem fated to hear it.

'Afraid not. All the conference bods must have stayed in tonight.'

'Ah, you've heard about the conference?'

'I read it in the paper. Still no idea what it's about.'

'It's a climate change thing. New solutions to old problems that won't go away. I won't go on about it, I don't want to put you to sleep prematurely.'

'So you're not here for two weeks of sun, sea, samba and Sambuca...?'

'... He said tactfully, leaving out the fifth *S*. No. Does it show?'

'I knew there was something different about you.'

'In a good way, I hope.'

24

'Your accent. I can't place it.'

'I moved around a lot as a kid. Armed forces dad, career soldier. Some of it's probably Irish, we were there for a long while. The rest – here and there.' I keep quiet and let her talk. 'Then I flew the itinerant nest and went to uni in England.'

'Where'd you go?'

'Cambridge. Went and never left.'

'I've never been.'

'Well, it's more of a concept than a place. Pretty, but also pretty unreal.'

'Sounds like you want to move on.'

'Ah, but I'm stuck in the Cambridge tech bubble, you see.'

She sips a little whisky from the bottle and the taste of the malt seems to set her adrift in thought. A frog somewhere in the trees behind the hut chirrups lustily. The mosquitoes are biting my ankles and I'm ready for my bed. Laura looks like she's itching to get back to her phone.

'Well, listen, I've gotta hit the sack, I'm knackered. Thanks for the drink. And try and get some sleep, yeah? If you're still here tomorrow, meaning later today, I'll see you...' I look at my watch under the Maglite. '... Sometime in the p.m.'

'We'll see. Maybe I'll still be around. Goodnight, Mike.'

I nearly tell her my name isn't Mike but what would be the point of that?

'Goodnight, Laura.'

I go back to my hut and get ready for bed. But before I turn out the light I open my notebook and pick up my pen and write down the next sentence of my book that I think might be true:

Laura is not who she pretends to be.

Six

I roll out of bed sometime around eleven. I forgot to switch the fan on before crashing out last night, and the mid-morning heat makes it impossible to sleep any more. I've had six hours. That's par for the course. I'm used to short nights and long tough days, I've had plenty of practice throughout my adult life.

On my way down to wash myself I pass Laura's hut, which is unsurprisingly locked up and quiet; she'll be zonked out with jet lag. At the bottom end of the compound, before it opens onto the shore, there are three private bamboo-walled shower-stands for the guests of Lily's Beach Huts. Today I have my pick of them so I step into the one nearest, latch the door, strip off my swimming shorts and soap the previous day's salt and sand and dirt out of my hair and off of my body. The cold water from the shower head is always a pleasant shock. When all the soap is rinsed off, I put my shorts back on and cross the last few yards to the sea for my morning swim.

In both directions the beach is bristling with sun umbrellas and covered with suntanned bodies of all shapes and sizes, the majority of them decorated with tattoos of varying ugliness or beauty. But the beach is quiet, too. No honking car horns, no pounding music, no drunken hysteria of the main drag. The belt of trees and buildings set along the beachfront efficiently insulates the beach from all that, even at night. Other than the odd whine of a distant ski jet there's only the squeals of delighted children at play, the inoffensive calls and laughter of a beach-volleyball game and the rhythmic plashes of my own body moving through the water. This quietness takes me by surprise, not just today but every day, because I never take it for granted. I like the quiet of the beach because it makes me feel safe where I am: away from all the claustrophobic noise and clamour back in the world I left behind.

I swim parallel to the shore, just far enough out for the water to be deep enough to avoid injury on dead coral. From there, looking back landward, I can see the tops of the wooded hills inland that rise behind the town, the highest and farthest crowned with a communications tower that winks a red warning light at night. I swim breaststroke from the front of Lily's Beach Huts to the front of the Aphrodite Snack Bar, about fifty metres south, then back again.

Once, I tried swimming out to the floating platform that people dive from and sunbathe on beyond where the waves start to form, but it was further than it looked. When I reached it I needed a rest but only managed to scrape my legs on barnacles as I tried and failed to lift myself onto the platform, and had to struggle back tired and grazed. If the platform hadn't been empty, I'd have swum back humiliated too. I'm not a strong or confident swimmer but the sea won't let me ignore it and keeps seducing me into believing it is something that can be mastered.

When I've swum enough I head back to the hut, towel myself dry and change into a clean pair of shorts, T-shirt and flip-flops before heading up to Lily's veranda for breakfast. This normally comprises a pot of coffee and a bowl of chopped fruit such as mango and pineapple; sometimes a croissant if I'm lucky or an orange juice if I'm good. Lily doesn't provide breakfast to guests but I've been a guest for so long I've become a resident, and making me breakfast has become a part of Lily's routine that seems to make her feel good about herself. She never talks about her past, a husband, kids, family, and I never asked her or anyone else about it. Her life seems as uncomplicated as mine, though I know that neither of them is.

'You ask lady about Shiri Palace last night?'

'Last night?'

'When you come back from working.'

So she knows Laura was still up when I got in, and that we talked.

'Lily, you don't miss a trick, do you?'

'Sleep with both eyes closed but keep one ear open.'

I nod and laugh.

'It's a conference.'

'I know it's conference. But why she go there and come back?'

'That, I don't know. If you're so interested, why don't you ask her yourself?'

'Because she not here.'

'What?'

'She go out early. Maybe two hour ago.'

'Did she check out?'

'No, just go out.'

I've finished my breakfast – no croissant this morning – and some undesirable bit of business is nagging me away.

'Listen, Lily, I gotta go. But... let me know when she gets back.'

'You be at Danny's later?'

'Sure. But phone me if she comes back before.'

'You gonna ask her about Shiri Palace?'

'I just wanna say goodbye before she goes off to her conference.'

'Okay, so maybe I ask.'

'You can do what you like, Lily. You're the boss. But go easy on her. Be nice.'

'You like her,' Lily says, grinning and pointing at me, taking the piss like I'm some lovelorn teenager.

I keep a straight face and reply, 'I like her money.'

That shuts her up and wins back her respect.

Seven

I leave the bike at home to save fuel. Where I have to go is only a ten-minute walk away from the busy main strip, up in the civic part of the town where the tourists only go if they've been robbed, lost their passport or are under arrest. I've never seen a tourist get arrested but I guess it must happen. The only time I see the police is on payola day, like today.

The guide books tell you there are no gangsters on the island but that's not quite true. Where America has its mafia to run 'protection' on small businesses and lone-wolf operators like me, here we have the police instead. Pay up on time and they'll leave you alone. It's just another inconvenient fact of life. I can live with it; at least I can for as long as I go on shelling out their weekly ten percent of my earnings. It's the only tax I have to pay, albeit a corrupt one, so I look on it as the cost of business, and it means I only have to worry about all the other robbers out there.

Inside the police station they keep me sitting and sweating in the airless hall for half an hour with a bunch of other reluctant patrons before I'm led down a corridor and admitted into Captain Bandura's office. It's cooler in there under his ceiling fan but the stink of sweat and old tobacco smoke impregnates everything in the room.

Bandura is sitting smoking behind his desk, wearing his customary short-sleeved police tunic with all its buttons and lanyards and shit. The cigarette hangs from between his lips: his leathery, gold-ringed hands are clasped on the desk in front of him. I've never seen Bandura from the waist down. He could be sitting with no trousers on and I would never know. I've never seen him anywhere doing anything other than smoking at his desk in this office while collecting his payoff. That's what he does. That's who he is.

'Busy week,' I say to him while he's counting the grubby notes I've just handed over. He folds the money into his breast pocket and looks up at me over his severe, nicotine-stained moustache. 'Mm?'

'What with the conference at Shiri Palace.'

'Oh, the conference. Yes. Good for you, no?'

'And for you. They must have security requirements.'

'They have their own security. We only go there if there's trouble.'

'Yeah, right.' The idea of the local police going anywhere where there's trouble is a first.

'How is Lily's Beach Huts doing?'

'I don't know. You'd have to ask Lily.'

'Oh, I will,' he says, as though suggesting some secret evil design. 'I'll see her soon. You can go.'

His eyes turn away from me to some bogus paperwork on the desktop. As I leave the room, the next poor sucker is sent in and Captain Bandura carries on with his busy day.

I step out of the police station into the sun-baked street. Overhead, where the sun is, the sky is bright and clear, but rain clouds are gathering out to sea and will soon scuttle in toward landfall. I take a route through the backstreets of the local market, rotten-smelling with butcher's blood and durian fruit, and come across five men trying to slaughter a large pig. I stop and observe from a few feet away.

The pig's plight is distressing but the physical efforts of the men to wrestle with it are comical to watch and for a while they make me forget about what just went on in Bandura's office. Then the scene ends with a knife drilled into the pig's throat and the comedy is over. I walk away to escape the sight of the blood draining out but the animal's frantic death-screams follow me down the street.

Sometimes, in the free hours between rising out of bed and starting work, I get on the bike and ride up into the hills just to see the views from up there, and look out for interesting wildlife. Birds, insects, lizards, monkeys. I keep a small pair of binoculars in the satchel for such occasions and sometimes make notes and sketches if I think something might be usable in a book one day. Because I'm conscious of the cost of fuel, it's been a while since I took the bike out for my own pleasure, but any idea of doing so today is scotched when the first fat drops of rain smack the dusty pavement. I quicken my pace in the direction of Danny's bar but by the time I get under the awning I'm as soaked as if I'd just stepped out of the sea, and the rain is vertically torrential to an intensity that only tropical rain can reach.

It's still too early for the first of the two small beers I allow myself before work so I order a coffee and sit at a table inside and take out my notebook and pen, listening to the rain rumbling on the roof. I leaf to the page I wrote yesterday and read what it says there:

Start with one true sentence, said Ernest Hemingway, and make it the truest sentence you know. Laura is not who she pretends to be.

That's not a bad opening. The first sentence affirms the truth of the second sentence and the second sentence introduces a character and creates suspense. I can change the name Laura to something else later. It looks like a pretty decent opening for a thriller or a mystery. Now all I need is a story.

I root around in my satchel and pull out a wad of dog-eared business cards bound with a rubber band. I remove the band and thumb through the cards, all from various hotels, resorts, guesthouses, campsites, until I find one for Shiri Palace. I take out my Motorola and punch in the telephone number printed on the card. A man at the other end picks up on the second ring.

'Shiri Palace reception. How can I help you?'

'I'm trying to contact a guest named Laura. I don't have a last name. Could you check if there's a Laura staying there for the conference, please?'

'No last name?'

'No, just Laura.'

31

I wait through a moment of silence, wondering what to say if he asks me who is calling.

'Just a moment, please.'

'Thank you.'

After a minute he comes back on the line.

'Mmm, I can't find no Laura. You sure you have the right name?'

'Okay,' I say, 'thanks for your help,' and hang up. I'm about to stow the phone back in the satchel when it rings in my hand. It's Lily.

'Hey You. Lady back. Gone in hut to change clothes.'

'Okay, thanks, Lily, I'll see you soon.'

Danny is fetching my coffee over. If Laura is changing into dry clothes she presumably isn't going out again any time soon in this weather. So I take my time and drink Danny's lukewarm coffee and make use of the loo before stepping back out into the downpour.

Back at the huts I see Laura sitting in the shelter of her veranda, her gaze alternately buried in her phone and looking up to enjoy the rain. She doesn't hear me approach because of the drip and gush of water all around us and I startle her when I step on to her porch. For an instant, I see fear in her eyes. It flairs briefly then cools to normal.

'Sorry,' I say. 'I nearly made you drop your phone.'

'You're soaked.'

'I'll dry out.'

'Here, sit down.'

I take the second chair and park my wet arse.

'Decided to stay, then?' I say.

'You know what? I have. I thought, fuck it, I'm happy enough here and it'll save my department a fortune in expenses. So I went and cancelled my reservation at the other place.'

'You've been up there, then?'

'Yes, sorry, I got somebody else to take me because I didn't want to wake you up.'

'Hey, no problem. Won't they miss you at the conference, though?'

'I can attend the conference just as well from here. It's only half an hour away. Is there a local bus?'

'I'll ride you there for free before I see you take the local bus.'

'Not good, huh?'

'Put it this way, it'd take two hours and drop you off half a mile away from the gates.' I'm shamelessly exaggerating somewhat.

'Right.' She turns back to the phone screen. 'Are you on Facebook, Mike?'

'Er, no.'

'Twitter, Instagram, anything?'

'I'm still stuck in the nineties, remember?' A thought comes over me and I nod at her phone. 'Can you do me a favour?'

'What?'

'Google a quote for me. Ernest Hemingway. Something about one true sentence.'

'Oh, I know it. It's from *A Moveable Feast*, if I'm not mistaken.' She types it in and finds something straight away. 'Here it is. Shall I read it out?'

'Sure. It's the bit about how to begin writing a story or overcoming writer's block.'

She reads the exact words from Hemingway's book. 'All you have to do is write one true sentence. Write the truest sentence that you know.'

So my opening sentence is almost 'true', and Hemingway's use of the comparative 'truest' confirms that he believed you can express gradations of truth. Maybe I shall make a good writer yet. But I still need a story.

'Is this for your novel?' asks Laura.

'Who said anything about a novel?'

'Your book, then.'

'Kind of, I guess. Writing's a slow process.'

'Well, don't stall. If you've got a beginning just keep writing and see where it takes you. You can always revise it later.'

'Thanks for the advice, Angela Lansbury.'

'Sorry. Am I being patronising?'

'I'm joking. You can probably tell that by now.'

I'm in no rush to be anywhere else and Laura seems in no rush to get rid of me so we sit with our feet up for a while, me staring at the rain, her typing with nimble thumbs on her phone.

'You said something up at Shiri Palace yesterday. You said "Shit, they're here already".'

Laura kills the screen and puts the phone down.

'I know. I'm sorry, I shouldn't have. It wasn't very professional of me.'

'Professional?'

'It's a work thing. Someone I wanted to avoid.'

'A competitor?'

'God, no. A colleague. Someone I have to work with, unfortunately. I didn't think he'd be here until Friday and I just couldn't face him before I'm forced to.'

'Right,' I say. 'Sorry to ask.'

'No, it's fine. I don't mind talking about it. Just not – in detail.'

'So it's just professional.' I'm pushing my luck now.

'It's – complicated.'

'Well if there's anything I can do to help…' I hear myself saying: whatever happened to not asking questions and not getting involved?

'Thanks, Mike. It's not a big thing, just two colleagues not seeing eye to eye.'

I say no more on the subject.

'You can't have had much sleep. Have you eaten?'

'I ate while I was out. I'm going to take a siesta very soon and not wake up until it's wine o'clock.'

'Well, keep your fan on. And light a mosquito coil when it gets dark. Lily'll be able to provide one if there isn't already one in the hut.'

'Thanks for the advice, Bear Grylls.'

I smile. 'Touché.'

The rain is still pounding down but I can't sit here all afternoon without looking like either a stalker or a needy puppy. I leave Laura to her nap time then pop into my hut to collect an umbrella before going out to get some lunch.

Eight

I eat a cheap plate of *nasi goreng* at a place for locals, away from the tourist-priced main strip, and wash it down with a bottle of lukewarm orange Fanta. The handful of other customers in there are watching their daytime soap on a small TV stationed above the counter but I have no interest in it so I sit and read my book for three quarters of an hour while the rain keeps lashing down outside.

The book I'm reading is an old Len Deighton Cold War thriller and the more of it I read, the more I think I've read it before. No offence to Len Deighton but quality literature is hard to come by in these parts. Most of what I read are books passed on by travellers, who tend to bring light holiday reading away with them, not *War and Peace*. Books are too expensive here for me to buy them new: foreign books sold in tourist shops are imported, and priced around the equivalent of fifteen or twenty dollars. I don't go in those shops any more in case I see a book that I'm tempted to shoplift, which would be wrong and a serious mistake if I got caught.

So I use the free book exchanges found in hotel foyers, guesthouses and 'traveller' hang-outs, which are invariably stocked with little but 'airport novels', most of them grubby and outdated as time advances and more and more tourists use a Kindle so that fewer new books come into the reading pool. Many of the books are in French, German, Italian or some language I don't even recognise, and therefore are of no use to me. Otherwise, I chance my luck among the romances, potboilers and whodunits, just to have a book on the go.

Recently, I thought I'd struck lucky when I picked up a novel by Thomas Pynchon, a name I recognised as a 'literary' author I might learn something from about writing; but thirty pages in there'd barely been a full stop and I had lost all track of what he was trying to say. I soon gave up on it after that. So I end up reading anything that tells a decent story, whether it's written well or badly, as long as I can understand it. It's a conscientious effort, I read mainly because I want to write, but I read out of long habit too because for half my life there was little else to do to pass the time.

When I look at my watch it's later than I imagined. I become aware that the rainstorm has passed and the sun is shining again. After paying for my meal I count how much cash I've got left on me. Then I stroll back to Lily's, letting my T-shirt and shorts dry in the sun, collect the bike and ride it to the nearest petrol station to fill up the tank, ready for later.

I spend the rest of the afternoon at Danny's as usual, chatting shit with him across the bar top, watching the beach fill up with bodies, brollies and beach towels and the masseuses setting up stall again after the rain, and drinking my two bottles of Singha. Then I check in back at Lily's before it's time to start work. She's sitting out on her porch enjoying the cooler air that the storm has brought, and a cigarette.

'Lady still here,' she says as I join her.

'She's staying. Didn't I tell you?'

'You see her, you tell her come pay for hut.' She points to a handwritten cardboard sign pinned up in reception that informs the guests of rule number one. 'Must pay in advance,' Lily quotes,'and she not pay me yet, only for one night.'

'Don't worry, Lily, I doubt she's gonna do a runner.'

'Damn right, she not do runner! I got copy of her passport.'

'When?'

'Today, when I see she going out without case. She leave case in hut. Mean she pay for one more day. Now you say she stay two more days, maybe more.'

'Okay, I'll remind her. Can I see the passport copy?'

Lily gives me a look of disapproval but nips inside reception, pulls the photocopy out of a drawer and brings it to me. The passport is only a year old and the photo ID is recognisably Laura down to the length of her hair. And I have a surname: Laura Duxton, no middle names. The date of birth puts her in her mid-thirties, three years younger than me. It's a United Kingdom of Great Britain and Northern Ireland passport and her nationality is recorded as 'British citizen', birthplace York. I fold the sheet of paper and hand it back to Lily.

'She conference lady?' asks Lily, as though I might have seen something in her passport details that she missed.

'I guess so. I don't know.'

'Maybe better we just mine our own business,' says Lily.

I keep telling myself that, and I don't know why I should care otherwise. Perhaps it's because of the way Laura retreated so quickly from the gates of Shiri Palace yesterday, or that brief but unmistakable fear in her eyes when I made her jump earlier, or just the simple fact of her travelling out here alone. She looks like someone in trouble. Like someone who needs someone to care. Or perhaps it's because I want her for my book, to see where her story can take mine. Once she's paid up for the hut, Lily won't care if she's a conference lady or at the top of the FBI's Most Wanted list. So it looks like it's down to me.

Nine

The island's airport is a small one, but busy. On the one hand, travellers are directed on foot between the aeroplanes and the arrival or departure hall, or are trundled around the flowery complex in cute little trolley trains. On the other hand, in high season there are scores of flights a day between here and the capital city on the mainland.

But all the flights are domestic only; no international flights touch down on the island. This I know from my taxi driver friends who work the airport trade. The domestic jets are smaller than international ones, carrying maybe a hundred passengers at a time. The flight from the mainland takes an hour – not much time to sleep and certainly no first- or business-class beds. It's unlikely that Laura switched flights, from international to domestic, straight to the island; she must have made at least one night's stopover somewhere, either in the capital or in her airline's gateway city between here and the UK, if that's where she flew from. That would account truthfully for her evident lack of jet lag. It represents the kind of detail that would look sloppy if overlooked in an otherwise well-plotted narrative.

I'm thinking about this in the back room of a little snack bar where Amnat, a cab driver who owns his own Volvo, and Kenny and Ralph, two fellow taxi cyclists, are joking and bantering over a card game that I walked in on. All three of them regularly tout for business at the airport, something I don't bother with, and they can't have been back long from their last run of the day. I order a coffee from May, the hostess, and sit down just as they're winding up the game. Amnat, not exactly the poorest of the three, is merrily raking all the crumpled notes to his end of the table. As I join them the conversation switches to English for my benefit.

'Hey, Mike,' says Kenny. 'You hear what happen up at Shiri Palace?'

'There's a conference. Something to do with the environment,' I say to him.

'Tell me about it,' says Amnat. 'Drove there and back ten times today. Lot of people from many different countries up there this weekend. Brunei, Australia, China...'

'Yeah,' Kenny interrupts, 'but you didn't hear? Some guy got hurt up there today. Helicopter ambulance came and flew him to the hospital. They say he fell from a balcony or something like that.'

'Who says?' I ask, not expecting a definitive answer.

'Word on the street. They say maybe he try to commit suicide. It made local news on TV but they didn't say much. Only his name and that he fallen.'

'What was the name?'

Kenny scrunches up his face and looks at me like I just asked him to wear a dress. 'Nnn, can't remember. Foreign name, western name. I didn't catch it right.'

'Is he dead?'

'I don't think so. Newsreader didn't say he died, just fell. They took him to main hospital other side of island.'

'When did the accident happen? What time?'

'I don' know. Some time in the morning, maybe.'

'Maybe he wake up still drunk,' Ralph chips in helpfully, 'or lose too much money in casino,' neither of which sounds like the behaviour of the kind of man who gets flown across the planet to attend a serious meeting about climate change.

Naturally, at the back of my mind is the thought that Laura could have been up there when it happened. According to what Lily said, she went out at around nine-thirty, ten, this morning, and Laura herself told me she went to the Palace to cancel her reservation; something she could probably have done over the phone. Maybe her being there and the man falling aren't connected, maybe it's a coincidence. But if she was there when it happened, surely she'd have known and ought to have mentioned it when I spoke with her this afternoon.

I'll have to get the story and the timeline straight before I go shooting my mouth off to her about it. Perhaps it didn't happen in the morning, perhaps it happened later, after Laura had been and gone. I can't make a story or an investigation or whatever the hell this is out of gossip and hearsay. I need to check the so-called facts of the matter, which means either going online at an internet café, something I never do, to look for updated news, or waiting for tomorrow's newspaper and hoping there'll be a report in there.

All of this becomes academic two hours later when I spot Laura sitting alone in the shade of a palm on the terrace of an upmarket bar overlooking a traffic-clogged junction on the strip. She's turned away from me, watching a gecko on the white wall behind her, and she has something colourful in a tall glass in front of her. I pull into a space and prop up the bike where I can see it then join her at the table.

'Do you stop and say hello to all your customers?' she says as I help myself to a chair.

'Only the interesting ones.'

'You can't get much work done that way.'

'Well, none of the others are ever that interesting.'

I shake my head at the waiter across the terrace and he acknowledges me as a tout doing business and leaves me alone, thinking I can't afford the bar's prices.

'And what makes me interesting?' she says. 'And I'm not fishing for compliments, by the way.'

'You're obviously clever, well-read and involved in this high-flown world of tech industries and international conferences, but you're not a snob.'

'O-kay…'

'And you're slumming it down here among all the riff-raff when you could be up there with all the VIPs enjoying the lap of luxury.'

'Mm-hm. A personal choice concomitant with your first observation.'

'What?'

'I'm not a snob. Perhaps I don't want to be up there with those people, doing what they're all doing.'

'Doesn't it look strange to them? Doesn't someone up there wonder where you are?'

'They know where I am.' Something or someone on the street catches her eye and what little colour there is in her face drains right out of it. 'Shit,' she says, lowering her voice and lifting a menu high in front of her, 'in fact, they're there now. Don't look.'

I do look, of course, though I don't know exactly who I'm looking at. Among the pavement crowd, a tall, distinguished-looking western man, dressed in loafers, slacks, a plain open-neck shirt and a linen jacket, walks by with a twenty-something attractive blonde in a pretty dress on his arm. Their heads swivel and crane at all the sounds and sights without turning our way. As they saunter on, bewitched by the hedonism of the town's nightlife, I nod at their backs and say:

'Who? Those two?'

'Oh, don't turn round, don't turn round...' Laura quietly chants at them until they are lost from sight in the crowd.

'Who are they?'

Laura lowers the menu and sighs with relief. After giving some thought to how much information she wants to feed me, she says, 'My ex.'

'Him or her?'

'Oh, very "woke". Him.'

'Ah,' I say. 'The colleague. No wonder you don't see eye to eye. Were you married?'

'No, but we were an item for years. He was my old research professor.'

'Or middle-aged, at least.'

'My, you are on form this evening. It's the typical story. He swapped me for a younger model. Now she's his sidekick, but we all have to work under the same aegis.'

'I don't know what that means.'

'It means I go and sit at the other end of the work canteen to them.'

'Right. Not exactly "professional", then.'

'Oh, please don't be a judgemental bore.' She looks at me seriously, long and straight into my eyes, for the first time.

'I'm sorry, that was very rude of me.'

'Don't worry about it.'

'No, really – '

'Apology accepted. Rudeness – intended or not – forgotten.'

'Can I buy you a drink?'

'Thanks, but I shouldn't,' I say. 'I'm on the bike. I should get back to work in a minute. Did you hear that there was an accident up at the conference venue?'

'Yes, I know, it's all over Facebook and Twitter.'

'I hope it wasn't anyone you know.'

'I know of him. Professor of Earth and Environment at Utrecht.' She reeled it off like something she'd just read on her phone.

'What are they saying about it on the internet?'

'That he's an Extinction Rebellion activist. That it was a publicity stunt. The usual lies, nonsense and conjecture.'

'Were you there when it happened?' I ask as casually as possible.

'No, it must've been after I left, otherwise I'd have noticed the kerfuffle. Apparently, the police were up there and everything.'

I try to imagine Captain Bandura venturing out from behind his cash desk and it doesn't work, I keep picturing him without trousers.

'It must put a downer on the conference mood. Are they still going ahead with it?'

'Good God, yes. Too much has been invested in it to call it off over one individual's unfortunate accident.'

'Was it an accident, though? I heard it might've been a suicide attempt.'

'Yes, well that's what they're implying with this publicity stunt angle. But I don't buy it. Pieter Visser's a sophisticated, intelligent human being, an academic, not a fanatic.' She reaches for her glass and sips the cocktail.

'You do know him, then?'

Does she blush ever so slightly or is it an effect of the heat and the drink?

'Only by professional reputation,' she says, then, as an afterthought, 'and from reading his journal papers.'

I go quiet for a bit, chewing it all over in my mind. Is it just me or does so much of this sound like bullshit? Then I say, innocently:

'Oh, Lily wants the rent in advance. She asked me to remind you.'

'Yes, of course. She'll have it in the morning. Unless you want to take it now.'

I register the sudden cold tone of that, and the implication that I'm only here doing Lily's bidding.

'Give it to her,' I reply.

Laura steers us back towards friendliness as if aware that she snapped at me out of turn. 'If I'm still up when you get back, you're welcome to come over for a nightcap on the veranda.'

I smile. 'I'd like that,' I say.

But later, when I get home, calling it an early night at three a.m., I find her hut locked and dark. I consider going back out to earn a bit more moolah before the last of the bars and clubs shut for the night, but instead I go back to my hut and sit out on my own porch and attempt, unsuccessfully, to squeeze out another sentence of the book I am trying to write.

Ten

The next morning I wake up earlier than usual and see Laura sitting out on her porch, dappled in tranquil sunlight. She's barefoot and wearing a wide-brimmed straw sunhat and a purple bikini, with a batik-print sarong wrapped around her lower half. Instead of the usual smartphone, she's reading an orange-spined paperback. The colouring of the jacket design identifies it to me straight away as a Penguin, a publisher with a reputation for marketing the kind of quality literature that I'm always looking out for.

'Morning,' I call out as I pass by.

'Morning. Where are you off to?'

'Down to the showers. Then for a swim. Want to come? Swimming, I mean.'

I wait and watch while she allows herself to say yes.

'Okay. I'll see you down there.'

I shower quickly and when I come out she's waiting for me at the fringe of the beach, minus the hat and sarong, and I can't help noticing that she has a tidy figure and lovely skin with no visible tattoos or scars. We wade out together and plunge into the shallow waves and I lead her through the warm water out to my usual distance.

'Watch your feet on the coral,' I say, treading water.

'It's dead here, isn't it?'

'Yeah,' I say. 'El Niño's a bitch.'

'Let's swim out to the raft,' she suggests. 'Or are you…?'

She means the anchored platform beyond where the waves start to form. Today I can see a couple of small upright figures on it.

'No, I'm fine, let's do it,' I tell her, and hope I'm not about to make a fool of myself.

She swims out ahead of me, executing a powerful front crawl against the inflowing current. After a minute, she stops and looks back, notes my slow and steady breaststroke, and treads water, waiting for me to catch up.

We arrive at the platform together and Laura hoists herself onto it straight out of the water with seemingly no effort. But half the strength has gone from my arms and stomach muscles and I dither and struggle as the current pulls my legs under the platform towards the dark, salty space where the sharp, nasty barnacles cling.

'Here.'

Laura reaches over and I grab her hand gratefully and she provides the other half of the strength I require to get a purchase and lever myself safely over the edge.

'Thanks,' I say, lying on my back in the sun, panting.

'You okay?'

'Never better.'

The other visitors to the raft are a couple of local kids playing hooky from school, if they ever went to school. The two boys, being about the same age, look more like friends than brothers. Both have deep-brown skin from being out in the sun every day and must be no more than ten years old, though most kids here look small and skinny for their age so it's hard to tell. They've been tumbling into the water and scrambling back out to plunge again all the time we were swimming out to them and their skin is wet and their hair is plastered to their heads. Laura says hello to them, and before she can ask them their names they are already bombarding her with cheeky grins and savvy sales patter.

'You come to Pyrotek tonight, cheap drink, loud music, special show for you. You come, have good time.'

'What's Pyrotek?' Laura says, turning to me.

'It's a club on the beach. You should go. They do put on a good show.'

'Yeah, you come, lady. Mike show you where.' The two lads dive-bomb back into the sea.

'Do you know these gentlemen?' says Laura, amused.

'They obviously know me. A lot of kids hang around the beach bars at night. And, without being racist, they all look pretty similar. I don't make a habit of encouraging them.'

'In what?'

'Hustling tourists.'

'As tempting as Pyrotek sounds, the conference begins in earnest tomorrow morning and I can't do a late night.'

'The fire dancers are worth a look, even if it's only for half an hour. They'll be there as soon as it gets dark.'

While she's pondering, the two giggling boys climb back onto the platform.

'Will you take me? Around, say, nine o'clock?' She's talking to me, not the boys.

'Sure. I'll meet you where you were last night, the posh bar on the corner.'

'You come tonight, lady, you come to Pyrotek,' the boys start in again.

'Yes, I'll come, I'll come,' says Laura, waving them goodbye before we both dive in and swim back to shore.

Back at Lily's Beach Huts, she invites me to stop by her veranda. 'I have something you might like,' she says.

'I'm intrigued.'

She picks up the Penguin book from where she left it lying on the table and offers it to me.

'I've finished it. It's not Hemingway but it's someone who I think is a better writer.'

I take the book and study the cover. *The Quiet American* by Graham Greene.

'I've heard of *The Thin Man*.'

'I think you mean *The Third Man*, darling,' she corrects me, putting an I'm-just-joking hand on my arm to forestall any class resentment on my part. She smiles and lets the touch linger for a little too longer than necessary.

'Thanks,' I say, lifting up the book in acknowledgement, giving her hand the chance to slide away naturally. 'What are you doing with the rest of your day?'

Before the Gulf

'I'm going to find a nice quiet restaurant where I can enjoy an expense-account lunch and sit and work quietly for a few hours. I need to tidy up my presentation for Saturday.'

'What time are you on? Maybe I'll come and listen.'

'Nothing would make me happier, Mike, I assure you, because it's ordinary people such as yourself that *should* be hearing all this stuff.' She sounds like a soapbox orator now. 'But I'm afraid it's for conference attendees only.'

I don't tell her I was only joking and I decide to ignore the 'ordinary' slur because she hasn't even noticed she's made it. In any case, I know what she means and that no offence is intended by it. Those delegates, or their sponsors, will have paid hundreds of pounds to be there, and will have paid it many months ago before even considering the added flight costs. And, unlike ordinary me, they are extraordinary, because the whole show will be couched in fancy jargon far beyond the understanding of the likes of me, who never got to go to Cambridge or any other university. Not that I'm bitter or anything, I only have myself to blame for that.

'No worries, I'm sure I'll find some other way to amuse myself,' I say, and wonder why ordinary everyday English so often comes out sounding smutty with innuendo. 'Don't work too hard this afternoon. I'm gonna go and read some Graham Greene.'

I start to depart but then stop and turn around at the stoop, like Columbo, with a cogent remark. 'Oh, yeah. *The Thin Man*… that's Dashiell Hammett.' I give her a knowing wink. 'I'll see you at the bar at nine.'

But I don't go and read Graham Greene. First, I go up to Lily's for my breakfast and to listen to her say, 'You late. Coffee go cold.' Then afterwards I take the bike and ride it up a narrow dirt road to visit my mate Panda at his shack in the hill forest.

48

Eleven

Panda, a big, friendly, slightly goofy-looking native islander, was one of the first people I met when I first washed up here. He migrated here sometime in the 1980s from the full-moon party island across the gulf when the rave scene over there got too notorious and tripped-out for his liking; so, like me, he began a new life here as an outsider. I met him in the days when he used to come down and peddle hash to tourists on the strip. He doesn't do that any more; nowadays he likes to keep himself to himself, hidden away like a hermit, and with good reason.

Panda hears my bike from down the track and steps from his shack, scattering feed grain to the chickens. His straggly hair is caught up in the posts of his wire spectacles, tugging them askew, the way Eric Morecambe fooled about with his, and a stout spliff of pure ganja is hanging from between his lips.

'Hey, brother,' he says to me as I prop up the bike and he comes in for a man hug. I told him a long time ago not to use my real name and he's always just called me 'brother' ever since. It's nice to have someone call me 'brother', though, technically, through the Mitochondrial Eve line, we are actually very distant cousins, like all the other human beings on the planet.

'Hey, Panda, how's it going?'

'Good, bro, good. Quiet, the way I like it. Wanna sit out an' drink a cold one together?'

'Sure, why not?'

'Then you can tell me what's on your mind.'

Panda disappears indoors to fetch the beers while I look at his paintings hanging on the outside walls of his shack. Brightly-coloured landscapes, plants, birds, all executed by his own hand. No human structures, no people in them, just natural formations and creations. Then I sit down on his grubby porch-lounger and gaze out at the surrounding forest. There's no view of the sea from here, only the banana trees, ferns and creepers of the encroaching wilderness. It's relatively cool in the perennial shade of the forest canopy but the mosquitoes are permanently active and the nearest shop is a bloody long way to go if you want a pint of milk.

While I'm waiting, I spot a pair of monkeys in a nearby tree, and take the binocs from my satchel to get a closer look at a parrot preening itself on a bough and a honey eater sending its curved beak into a flute-like flower in the bushes close by. Flashes in the binocular sights turn out, when I lower the binocs, to be clouds of yellow butterflies, as yellow as flying daffodils, and I realise they're all around me.

'You want some o' this, brother?'

Panda puts down two tins from the fridge and sits next to me on the lounger and takes the spliff from between his lips and holds it out to me.

'Nah, I'm good, thanks. I'll take the beer, though.'

He puts the cold tin in my hand. I'll have to account for this one later at Danny's if I'm going to work tonight.

'You sell any?' I say, shooting a thumb at the paintings behind us.

'Some. Private buyers. I don't have no sign up here or anything, you know?' We crack open the tins together. 'Long time, brother, long time,' he reflects.

'Yeah. I've been busy.' I feel bad saying that, it's a shitty line, but it's true and I can be honest with Panda without dressing it up. 'You know what it's like down there. The daily grind.'

'That's why I built myself this place.' He throws his thumb over his shoulder at the ramshackle house. 'Get away from all that rat race.'

'I bet you still have rats up here.'

'Yeah, just not the human kind.'

Panda has reached that age when he's happy to take a step back from the world and let it go on its mad way without him.

'Mister Sociable, eh?'

'I still got my contacts.'

'I know.'

'I'm connected to the world. Got the genny and my computer up and running. All the mod cons I need, brother.'

'Well, good on ya.'

We shut up and tap beers and take a long pull on them.

'So is this a business call?' Panda asks.

'Could be. You still do ID work?'

'You know it, brother. Come inside, take a look.'

Inside, Panda's house is a sweatbox and smells mildewed, imbued with the fertile environment of the jungle, but it presents a certain Hobbit-like charm and cosiness to the eye. Panda leads me to a small room, curtained from daylight, in the back where a fancy-looking camera on a tripod is set up to point at a white roller-screen. Beyond this room is a doorway to a further burrow-like windowless recess where I can just about see plastic flasks of chemicals on wall-mounted shelves and various items of darkroom equipment.

'Whatever it is you want, bro, I can do it right here.' Panda stretches his arms wide like Frank Sinatra taking a standing ovation at Carnegie Hall.

'You sure this place is sufficiently ventilated?' The air smells acrid with developing fluid or some shit.

'Trust me. It's my own architectural design. This place is plenty ventilated. And in case of emergencies, I even got a mask.'

He reaches up to a shelf in a dark corner and pulls down a gas mask that looks like it belongs in World War Two.

'What you want?'

'You hear of a climate conference at Shiri Palace this weekend?'

'No.'

'Well there is,' I say. 'And I want a pass to get into it. Can you make me one?'

'You know what one looks like?'

It's my turn to say no.

51

'That's tough, man. If you can get me one, I can copy it, sure. Otherwise…'

'If I could get one I wouldn't need one.'

I think about trying to 'borrow' Laura's pass without her knowing, then I think about how stupid and dangerous that would be.

'They got press there? Because I can make you up a press pass, no problem.'

I don't know if the press would normally be invited to such a conference. It looked, from what I gleaned from the newspaper article, like the sort of event that only gets reported in academic journals. But what with the professor falling from the balcony, this conference isn't normal any more and has made the news already. There must be plenty of reporters snooping around up there, looking for the real story. Will anyone notice one more?

'You know what,' I say, 'that could work.'

'When you need it for?'

'Tomorrow morning.'

Panda looks at his watch. 'Come back this afternoon, around four o'clock. I can have something for you by then. And be ready to get photographed.'

'Okay. But all copies to me.'

'Of course.'

'How much?'

'For you, fifty dollars.'

This is madness but fuck it.

'Okay,' I agree, and we shake hands on the deal.

Twelve

Back in town, I go to the bank for the first time in two years. The last time I drew money out was to bump up the cash that I needed to pay for the Honda Click. It was a big deal and I had to talk with my mother on the phone to persuade her to authorise the payment. That was the last time we spoke, and she wasn't happy about it. Luckily, this time, a couple of hundred pounds is not a significant enough amount to trouble her over, though no doubt some statement will eventually flop through her letterbox and cruelly remind her that I still exist in the world.

I convert the currency and set aside Panda's money for the fake press pass. Then I go to a backstreet clothes store and pick out two short-sleeved shirts of markedly different colours, proper ones with buttons and a collar, a pair of beige cotton trousers and an appropriate-looking lightweight neutrally-coloured jacket. Then I visit a shoe shop and buy a pair of tan moccasin-style shoes. I take this lot back to my hut and go into the back to shave before putting on the new outfit.

Once I'm ready, I sneak back out to the bike, hoping Lily is nowhere to be seen, not wanting to provoke her curiosity with my new togs. At reception, I remember Laura's passport photocopy in that drawer, just a few feet away. I step inside lightly, trying not to rock the floorboards, and the drawer slides open quietly. I pull out the document, push the drawer shut again and get the hell out of there.

Back up at Panda's shack, I show him the photocopy.

'What do you think? Could this be a fake passport?'

He takes it to a desk and puts it under a huge mounted illuminated magnifying glass, tilting it this way and that in the electric light.

'Nothing stands out as fake. Hard to say for sure, though. The background design hasn't copied good enough to tell anything.' He hands it back. 'Who is she?'

'She's staying at Lily's. Here for the conference. But there's something about her. Stuff that doesn't add up.'

'When I say "who is she?" I mean, why is it your problem?'

I find myself reluctant to mention that I'm writing a book and looking for a good story. It sounds lame. I don't want Panda to think that I regard myself as 'a writer'. It would be phoney. So I make something else up.

'It isn't,' I say instead. 'Maybe I'm just bored.'

'And this has nothing to do with the guy who fell out the window over at Shiri Palace?'

'I thought you didn't know about the conference.'

'I didn't. I looked it up after you went.'

'I dunno. Maybe it does, maybe it doesn't.'

'Aw, come on, brother, what's your angle in all this?'

'I'll tell you when I find out.'

'Well, you look the part, Mister Journalist,' he says, eyeing my new threads up and down, and noticing the smoothness of my chin. 'Please step this way.'

He positions me in front of the white roller-screen and I gaze as blandly as I can into the camera while he takes half a dozen shots. It's the first time I've let myself be photographed in years and it feels weird trying to look natural and... unthreatening.

'So who am I?' I ask afterwards, while Panda unscrews the camera from the tripod.

'Oh, yeah.' He leads me to the desk and shows me the pass, with the paper's masthead logo on it and a space where he will attach my photo. 'Bob Lorrimer,' he says, '*Singapore Straits Times*.'

'Fucking hell, that's a bit upmarket, isn't it? I thought it was gonna be a local rag.'

'Ain't no Englishmen working on them small island papers, bro. Anything else, they'll smell a rat.'

'All right. Bob Lorrimer. Bob. At least you gave me a nice easy name to remember. Is there a real Bob Lorrimer?'

'Oh, yeah. He's real, all right. But he's a janitor over there at the paper. One of my agents in the field.' Panda winks and I don't know whether he's making this up or being serious. 'If the whole thing blows back, Bob's there to take a bullet for the team. He won't say nothing, not even under torture. Got a special cyanide tooth. He'd rather die than give away the identity of some taxi cyclist trying to blag his way into some academic symposium...'

'All right, all right, I get the picture.'

He got me going then, but I have to admit his English is very good when he lets it take flight.

'Now let me get on with this thing.'

Panda shuffles away into the darkroom, taking his gas mask with him, and I go to wait outside among the paintings, butterflies and mosquitoes, and drink my second beer while he develops the prints. Beer number two: no visit to Danny's bar today. By the time Panda's finished, the sun has gone down, all the butterflies have gone away and I am getting bitten to fuck. But I have a convincing press pass in my hand and Panda has fifty dollars in his, which by local rates isn't bad for an afternoon's work.

I head back to town and am nearly all the way there before it hits me that I forgot to take the contact strip with the rest of those photos of me on it. I figure I'll pick it up later or that Panda will destroy it.

I go back to Lily's to change out of the overly-warm clothing and into my work strip. I hang around the site for ten minutes waiting for Lily's back to be turned so I can replace the photocopy in the drawer. Whatever I intended to prove by its removal is inconclusive. I walk around to the bike and get to work at squeezing a few jobs in before it's time to meet Laura.

Thirteen

I swing the bike past the posh bar at the junction a little before nine and Laura is already sitting out on the terrace at the same table as before; a creature of habit, maybe, or someone with a need to establish routines. The terrace is busy, all the other tables and seats taken, and she looks like she's holding on to the last free chair for me. I park the bike and join her.

'Hey, thanks,' I tell her, and grab the chair just as her resolve is about to crumble.

I try not to think about the skulking I've done behind her back today, nosing into her passport details and showing them to Panda. I need to 'act natural' and not reveal that I know anything about who she is, or isn't.

'It's busy tonight,' she says, looking at the edgy traffic and manic crowds clogging up the strip.

'The weekend approacheth.'

'Can I buy you a drink? Oh, the bike…'

'Let me get you one,' I say, and signal the waiter over before she has time to protest.

'Oh. A white wine spritzer, then, please. If you're sure.'

'And I'll have a blackcurrant and soda water.'

The waiter moves towards the bar, picking up more orders on the way.

'So,' I say, 'you ready for the big day?'

'Oh. Tomorrow. Ready enough.'

'What time you on?'

She hesitates. Is she visualising the timetable of events or generating a random number? Her mind should be quicker than this. Or maybe she just doesn't want to tell me.

'Twelve,' she says eventually.

'Isn't that lunchtime?'

'Lunch is one till two. I'm the last speaker of the morning in one of the rooms – I forget which one,' she adds before I can ask.

'What's it about? Your presentation.'

'Clean-up of micro-plastics at the source, in the rivers and sewers, before they can get into the ocean.' She reels it off assuredly, like she's said it a thousand times before, which she would have done in her business.

'Sounds important.'

'Yeah. Very. Plastic is the biggest problem facing this planet right now, and... And I told myself I wouldn't talk shop when I'm out trying to have a good time.'

Our drinks arrive and we manage to make issue-free small talk while we finish them. She asks me how the writing is going and I tell her I've got nearly three sentences. I ask her about what she does in Cambridge and she names some tech firm I've never heard of which she tells me has just been bought up by the Chinese for twenty billion dollars, and I say that most of the world's giant companies nowadays are owned by happy men of the east, that at least I know, so nothing new there.

When the drinks are drunk, I call for the bill and pay with a generous tip out of what's left of the bank withdrawal I made this afternoon. Then Laura climbs on the back of my scooter and I take her to see the fire show before it reaches her bedtime.

Fourteen

We have to leave the bike on the street and walk a narrow alleyway that takes us to the beach, like stepping through a portal into a tropical fairyland. It's darker here, and cooler from the night-time sea breeze. It's quieter than the street too, but not as distantly drowsily peaceful as it is in the daytime. The night compresses sound. The beachfront bars and restaurants have set out their stalls for the supper trade and the rumble of human conversation flattens and diminishes the rhythm of the sea. We walk along, guided by twinkling garlands of lights and fielding many imprecations to 'come dine with us' as we go.

We hear Pyrotek unmistakably quite a way before we can see it. It's the swelling sound of pumping house music overlaid with a wailing tenor saxophone. And a lot of people having a fucking good time.

The fringe of the crowd begins some way from the frontage of the venue and the press of bodies thickens as we weave our way closer to the main action. The front of Pyrotek is a white, two-terraced façade of vaguely art deco design, trimmed in neon and bristling with lasers. Spotlighted behind a safety rail up on the roof, like the captain at the helm of the Love Boat, is the man making all the noise with the saxophone, and on the raised ground-level terrace, mixing the beats, is the young female superstar DJ flown in a week ago from Berlin.

Most of the people around us are young and western and dressed with no more than beach decorum, the party being an extension of a day of sun-worshipping.

'Wow, this is awesome,' says Laura, gripping my arm so as not to lose me in the milling of the crowd. 'I thought there'd be an entrance charge or something.'

'You can't make people pay to be on the beach. Well, not here, anyway. Only in places this lot can't afford to go.'

When we look down to find our footing we see a few perky-looking dogs trotting through the forest of bare legs, eager for scraps or attention. Then we are looking down at the two young boys from the raft this morning, ferreting out of the throng, both wearing Day-Glo deely-boppers.

'Hey!' cries Laura in delight.

'You buy wand?' The boys are waving armfuls of Day-Glo toys and don't recognise her at first. Then they see me with her and remember us from the raft. 'You buy wand, lady, you buy wand! You say you come buy wand.'

A Day-Glo flying saucer whizzes up like a providential sign into the dark sky and, before Laura's got her money out to buy a length of plastic crap to wave to the beat of the music, there are five or six other kids crawling out of the legwork to sell us shells, carvings, coins and whatever other merchandise they got their hands on today.

'Come on,' I say, taking hold of Laura's hand, 'let's find a place to sit.'

'Yes, please.'

The patio area in front of the club is also busy but less so. Most people have just been drawn by the party, the music and the surrounding buzz, but if you take a seat here it means you buy a drink, and the prices aren't cheap and the waiters are keen and alert. It gives us a respite, though, and a good spot to view proceedings from. The beach pedlars won't bother us here, they know they'll get chased off before they can make a sale.

It's been five hours since my last beer, up at Panda's, and I figure it won't hurt to have one more now. Laura asks for a small glass of red wine. The waiter, a guy in a scarlet jacket, brings the drinks. To no surprise looking at the open chaos around us, he asks apologetically for cash or card on delivery.

'I'll get these,' says Laura, and hears no argument from me.

'Ah, look! Down there.'

I stand up, looking towards the sea, and urge her to do the same. Over the heads of the crowd we catch brief dazzling arcs of whirling white fire.

'Let's go down,' Laura says. 'Can we take our drinks?'

'Sure.'

We shuffle past bodies down to the edge of the space surrounding the performers. Two young local men – boys, really, probably still in their teens, dressed like extras from a *Mad Max* movie in black leather and straps and rapper-style baseball hats – wield their sets of burning swing-clubs with mind-boggling skill and coordination. The fires behave like giant sparklers, tracing complex shapes and patterns in the air which only our slow human eyes can see. The dance of fire follows in time to the music. At the drop, when the beat fades, builds and kicks back in, the jugglers slingshot the chain-handled clubs high, high up into the air and catch them effortlessly, drawing the fire back into the swift-flowing river of the routine.

It makes me think of all the thousands of hours they must have practised this, suffering not just accidents and frustration but also unimaginable boredom stretched to the outer limits of pointlessness, letting it invade their sleep and control their lives, essentially sacrificing themselves, all to create these fleeting moments of supreme beauty.

When their fuel burns out they walk off to the cheers of the crowd and two other lads take their place in the arena. These two are more traditionally dressed. Short lads, naked down to the waist then clad in silk costume pantaloons, they look like extras from the *Mahayana*, minus the monkey masks. Their weapon of choice is a pair of two-foot batons, one in each hand, set alight along most of its length. The dancers swing them like clubs and find a rhythm that engages us then suddenly switches as they turn their bodies about-face, sending the fires rotating in opposite orbits. As the dancers twirl, they whip the columns of fire around their bodies like nunchaku in a kung-fu display. Then the batons are lifted aloft and made to resemble a single staff blazing at both ends, like Darth Maul's doubled-ended light-sabre swashbuckling death and destruction.

'They're amazing,' says Laura, holding her phone aloft and snapping pics on it.

'Yeah,' I say, and point out to sea: 'Look out there.'

About ten metres from the shore, two people waist-deep in the water are completing the construction of a scaffolding platform that reaches three metres in height above the waves. As they finish the task and wade back, a third lad, this one well-built, by far the burliest of the troupe, replaces them, trudging out through the water, his apparatus slung from his shoulder, and climbs up the cross-poles to take his position on the planks.

Laura stares in wonder, keeping her questions to herself, waiting to see what will happen next.

The lad out on the platform sets light to two globes and takes up an Olympian stance. Working first his arms, then his shoulders, his upper torso and finally his hips, bringing all the parts of his body into common step, he swings the fire globes at first like thuribles, creating wider and wider arcs as he feeds out the lengths of chain, until they are turning vertically into each other in complete circles, like the hypnotic revving up of some Howard Hughes-sized aircraft propeller. As the balls of fire spin, they emit jet-trails of sparks, creating a giant Catherine wheel effect. The faster the dancer spins, the farther and higher the sparks spiral up into the night, ten, twenty meters, fanning out to a peacock's tail of light. After no more than two minutes, the fires fade and die. But one small moment in time has been magically illuminated and celebrated.

'Oh, my God, that was incredible,' says Laura, letting go her breath.

'Glad we didn't miss it.'

There are new dancers and jugglers performing in the beach arena now, and everyone's attention turns away from the lonely titan of the waves dragging his chains back to shore. I've seen all these tricks a dozen times before, of course, but I stick around, letting Laura's enthusiasm have its free reign, at least until my beer is through.

The performers, sensing the rise of the crowd's excitement, start inviting and encouraging audience participation, and one young blonde girl in denim shorts and a sparkly bikini top immediately presents herself as the object of every male gaze with a good enough view.

The juggler positions himself close behind her, taking great care not to show any sexual impropriety, and brings his arms round to weave his two rotating maces into a wheeling donut of fire six inches before her eyes.

The grin on the girl's face is huge but nervous. Her instinct is to lean backwards away from the fire, and the dancer leans back behind her and the fire follows them. When he whips it safely away, the liberated girl turns and squeals with delight at her posse of friends.

Laura shows me a photo she captured of the fire wheel and the look on the girl's face. Then she pulls me next to her and holds the phone-cam at arm's length to take a selfie but I pull away before she can tap the button.

'No, sorry.'

'But Mike…' She thinks I'm kidding.

'Sorry but I'm just one of those people who don't like their photo taken.'

Thankfully, she doesn't insist or act offended, and changes the subject once we finally move away to a quieter spot.

'I've seen fire jugglers at festivals before, but never anything like that.'

'Yeah? I didn't have you down as the festival-going type.'

'Right, so I'm a type, am I?'

'I had you down for a boffin. I didn't know boffins did anything but boff.'

She can see I'm just making fun of her, it shows on her face.

'I've been to Glastonbury, once. And the Strawberry Fayre, of course…'

'Isn't that the Beatles?'

'Fuck off,' she laughs, 'you know it isn't.'

I don't tell her that I've barely heard of those places, never mind been to them.

As she finishes her wine, I see her look at the time on her phone and I realise this pleasant interlude is about to end and I shall soon have to get back to work on the strip.

We follow our trail back up the sands towards the access alley where I left the bike, and the noise of the party fades behind us as we rerun the gauntlet of beachside restaurateurs.

When we recover the bike, I drop Laura off at Lily's and wish her good luck for tomorrow. As we say goodnight, she leans in with her hand on my shoulder and kisses me on the cheek.

'You shaved,' she murmurs.

'Yeah. I do that sometimes.'

She steps back and I shake the moment away inside my head.

'So, Shiri Palace. What time d'you wanna leave?'

'Oh. It'll be early. Obviously, there are other presentations I want to see before mine.'

'Obviously. Well, that's all right, I can do early. I can always come back and have a siesta.'

'Well, let me give you a knock in the morning and see if I get a response. Then I'll know it's not too early.'

She is being evasive about time again but I don't push it and we leave it at that.

Later that evening, though, I decide to stop work early and call it a night. The remainder of the cash I took out of the bank will tide over the loss of earnings. So around eleven I go back to the hut and clean my teeth and crawl into bed to get an early jump, one way or another, on tomorrow's conference.

Fifteen

In the night I dream about Cory Stewart for the first time in a long while.

Cory was an older boy I knew in the place where I grew up as a kid. We hung out together, played football, got into mischief, went wandering the hills and fields and exploring the local woods together. I don't really know why he chose to hang out with me, not at first. It's not like we were in the same school year. But, for a long while, I thought he was my best friend.

The main street through the home village of my childhood is where the dream unfolds, though the topography is distorted, caricatured, the way it always is in the ever-changing, never-changing world of dreams. All the neighbourhood kids are outdoors, lined up along both sides of the main road as if for a royal visit. Their hidden faces are all turned in one direction, away from my viewpoint, watching and waiting for something or someone to appear along the empty byway.

Then they begin to clap in unison, and stamp their feet, and then they begin their chant: 'Cory Stewart's coming back, Cory Stewart's coming back, Cory Stewart's coming back…' Over and over, to the tune of 'London Bridge is falling down', like a stuck record, or an eerily cheerful incantation.

But the road remains empty.

Suddenly, the children are gone, the village is gone, the intervening years are gone, and Cory is here, in the night-time silence of my hut, sitting cross-legged at the foot of my bed with one of his eyes watching me sleep on the other side of the mosquito netting.

I open my eyes and the room is light and Cory looks just the way he did the last time I ever saw him. Staring at me through one eye.

I wake up for real, sweating, expecting it to be morning, but when I scrabble between the mattress and the mosquito net for the Maglite and check my watch it is still the middle of the night.

I bury my head in the pillow and try to shake off the dream, willing Cory Stewart not to come back again. After ten minutes, I switch the torch back on, reach for my notebook and write down what's on my mind. Then I can sleep again.

Sixteen

In the morning the open notebook is on the floor over the edge of my bed. I read what I wrote there in the night and realise that I have my three sentences now.

Start with one true sentence, said Ernest Hemingway, and make it the truest sentence you know. Laura is not who she pretends to be. But I think I know who she might be.

I reach down and flip the notebook shut. I don't have time to lie around thinking cute ideas about truth. Instead, I turn my mind to strategy. If I wear the new clothes to ride her to the conference they are bound to ping on Laura's radar, and I don't want to make her think anything unusual is going on so I'll have to ride her out to the venue then come back and change before returning as Bob Lorrimer of the *Singapore Straits Times*.

The plan to impersonate a reporter doesn't sit easily. I've no idea what to expect there, how I'm going to act or what I'm going to say. I don't even know why I'm doing this; or if I do I won't admit it to myself yet. I try to keep thinking of my book. That's what I'm doing: creating a narrative, even if only of my own folly, on which to hang all those one true sentences. This motive only rings half true any more, but whatever happens it will be an adventure beyond the daily grind of ferrying drunken tourists up and down the strip then going back to my empty beach hut.

But when I knock on Laura's door at eight-fifteen there's no response. While I'm listening for a sound inside, Lily shouts down from the house:

'SHE GONE. WENT EARLY.'

I walk up to her through the trees to stop her from pissing off those occupants still sleeping, and because I don't want everyone to hear our business.

'She say sorry, din't wanna wake you after long night working. I tell her you go bed early but she go anyway.'

'Did you see who took her?'

'You mean I follow her out onto street? No!'

'Okay. Thanks, Lily.'

She beckons me to stay a moment.

'You interested in this girl, no?' Lily arches her eyebrows but there is no accompanying uplift of the mouth, nor any sign of encouragement in those brown, milky eyes; only censure, a mixture of cruelty and sadness. 'Why? Why you no keep quiet life? Keep head down, work, stay out of trouble with tourists, like a good boy.'

'I've never been in trouble with a tourist,' I say, keeping an even tone and a straight face, trying to show her the respect I know she deserves, even though her sudden interference angers me on some level.

'Until now,' says Lily. 'I don't have good feeling about her. She spell trouble. You should stay away.'

'I want to know who she is and why she's here,' I state more forcefully than I intended to.

'We know why she here. She here for conf'rence. Who care why she book out of big fancy resort? She like it here, that's all. Or maybe you think she here because she like you.'

'That's not it. It's that she lied about how she came here. No taxi driver mistakes this place for Shiri Palace or ditches a fair just like that. That's bullshit. They all understand English.'

'So she lie about that. Maybe driver say something rude to her and she got out but din't wanna say the reason. But you right 'bout one thing. If she lie, you can't trust her. That's why you should stay away.'

Even my excuse that I'm collecting material for a book abandons me as I struggle to respond. Lily's advice, however intrusive, is sound, and I should take it. But I'm working on instinct alone now.

'I need to know why.'

'Why what?' Lily sighs.

'I'll tell you when I know.'

As I walk away to the hut to change, Lily delivers her parting shot at my back.

'You be careful. And don't do nothing bad or stupid!'

Seventeen

I change into the new outfit, making sure to wear the other shirt to the one I'm wearing in the photograph on the fake press pass. I ride the bike as far as the turnoff road up to Shiri Palace then park it in the shade of a bush and go the last hundred metres on foot. I take the walk slowly, trying not to build up too much of a sweat. I want to arrive looking like I've just stepped out of an air-conditioned taxi. At least it isn't raining, though I should've brought an umbrella, for shade. At the gates, I'm feeling more than a little sticky, but dithering in the sun will only make it worse. I enter the grounds and head for the front doors.

The main building, surrounded by well-tended grounds scattered with similarly-styled guest bungalows and outhouses, is a five-storey stone structure that looks a little like a Japanese castle – white walls and a mountainous roof mantle of rippling aquamarine porcelain tiles. As I approach, I don't even think about showing my 'press pass' without someone asking to see it first. 'Offer nothing, act normal, don't overcompensate,' I tell myself. My hand twitches towards it at the sight of the uniformed doorman but he opens the door for me and steps back without question, just a polite 'Good morning, sir' in English. I smile and step into the air-conditioned coolness of a spacious, high-ceilinged lobby.

Framed by a double staircase to the upper floors, a big banner announces 'Welcome to the 5th ASEAN State of the Environment Symposium'. I've never heard of ASEAN, unless it's a misspelling of 'Asian', which would be pretty appalling if they couldn't get that right. I don't know if there's a difference between a conference and a symposium, but if there is then Panda's English is better than mine and maybe he should be writing this book.

Beneath the banner is the grand doorway entrance to the conference proper, red-roped off and staffed by a couple of security guys, one beefy in a tight suit, the other skinny in one that hangs loosely. Through the entranceway, I can see women and men, the majority of them Oriental, in formal dresses and business suits, some holding teacups and saucers, milling and talking in a long chandeliered hallway. Along its length, other doorways lead to side chambers, presumably where the multiple presentations are being given. But, unless my presence just hasn't been queried yet, the reception area I'm standing in is evidently open to the public, several members of which are perusing a range of exhibits.

A quick glance tells me Laura isn't out here where she could easily spot me and wonder what I'm doing here. I can't see her among the crowd through the doorway either so she must be in one of the side rooms listening to somebody's talk. I'm only imagining how these things are organised. But it's funny she never mentioned this public exhibition when I suggested I might come along to her speech and she trumpeted the opinion that people like me are the ones who *should* be receiving the message. When I put this together in my head, it hits me with a what-the-fuck moment.

A glass display case catches my eye and I amble across a few metres of polished marble floor to see what's inside. It turns out to be some kind of artwork, a circular mosaic the size of a fifteen-inch pizza, tightly packed with battered-looking fragments and small objects: buttons, rings, bottle-caps, key-ring ornaments, cigarette lighters, bits of tubing, bits of insulated cable flex, a plectrum, a crucifix and a topping of other stuff too worn down, chipped or mangled to identify.

I catch a reflection in the glass of a blonde woman in a dress joining me at the display. I don't know if she's a tourist or a delegate or whether she speaks English or not, but I came here to find out something so I might as well jump in.

'What am I looking at?' I say aloud without looking up from the mosaic.

'Plastic,' she says. 'Horrible, isn't it?'

I raise my head and recognise her at once but don't say anything; I know I'm safe. Then I twig about the display.

'Is this from inside a shark or something?'

'I wish.' Not what I expect to hear from an environmentalist. 'A shark's stomach can contain that much without the animal dying. What you are looking at is from the stomach of an albatross chick.'

She speaks English with a slight accent, German maybe or Danish, and I put her in her mid-twenties, like the last time I saw her. I register my genuine surprise at what she has just told me.

'No way!'

If I gathered up all the detritus in the case there would be several fistfuls. So how big is an albatross chick's stomach? The woman leans her head to one side, giving me a quizzical look.

'You're not with the conference, are you?'

'No.' I wonder if this is the time to introduce my journalist alter-ego but some inner wisdom holds me back. 'Just a visitor.' I take a chance. 'I'm Robert Lorrimer. Bob.'

She reaches out a hand and takes the bait.

'Hi, Bob, I'm Kristina. So, you wanna save the world?'

My answer is deliberately glib.

'Who doesn't?'

Her laughter of incredulity almost bowls her over.

'Well, there are plenty, Bob. Governments like the United States and China. Trans-national corporations. In fact, the list is pretty long.'

To avoid getting in over my head, I distract her from a debate by asking about the large TV screens, eight of them spaced around the edges of the room, showing montages of natural phenomena like the sea, forests and ice masses.

'Come, take a look.'

She leads me across the room to a screening of a two-minute video called *Harrison Ford is The Ocean*. We watch and listen to the actor give voice to the ocean itself. Its

71

warning to the human race is chillingly delivered: 'I don't need you but you need me.' When the show is over Kristina moves me on to the next screen, which is showing *Julia Roberts is Mother Nature*. We watch and listen for a moment before curiosity draws me on round all the others. *Liam Neeson is Ice. Penélope Cruz is Water. Joan Chen is Sky. Edward Norton is The Soil.* A couple of actors I've never heard of are Coral Reef and Forest. All eight videos have the same expensively filmed visual design and the same collective warning from the big Nature: I don't need you but you need me. As a set, they represent an impressive and efficiently branded product.

'You notice who's missing?' says Kristina.

'Volcanoes?'

'No!' she laughs. 'Which actor?'

I can't begin to guess.

'There are actually nine films in the whole sequence but ASEAN refused to show the ninth.'

I still have no idea.

'It's Kevin Spacey. He voices The Rainforest.'

I know I'm looking blank. A journalist would know this shit.

'You know who Kevin Spacey is…?'

'I've heard of him.' I try to recall movies I've watched in tourist bars from Krabi to Ubud, and come up with one. '*The Usual Suspects*! Wasn't he in that?'

'Well, yeah, but, you know…'

'What? He isn't dead, is he?'

'No! You really don't know, do you? About the sexual harassment allegations. Hollywood kicking him out. All that stuff.'

I cover myself awkwardly. 'Celebrity news isn't my thing.'

'So what is your thing? You're not a tourist, are you?'

'What makes you say that?'

'The way that you evade the question.'

I have to tell myself that she isn't flirting and make a decision.

'I'm with the *Straits Times*.'

'Oh. So you *are* here for the conference. Please, come this way.'

Before I can stop her she crosses the lobby with me in tow to the reception desk and speaks to a young female receptionist, who reaches under the desk and passes her an iPad.

'Bob Lorrimer, Bob Lorrimer,' she mutters, scrolling down the screen. Then she looks up and I realise I've blown it. 'It says Gail Riviera is covering it for the *Straits Times*, and she's already here.'

'Yeah, that's what I was about to tell you. I'm not here for the conference, I'm here on a different story. The accident yesterday involving one of the delegates. I'm freelance.' I don't know why this last touch should persuade her of my general honesty and decency when it could equally increase her suspicion. I'm overcompensating, damn it.

'Ah. Professor Visser's accident.' I sense a wall go up: the flirting that never happened is now over. 'Do you have ID?'

I slip the press card out of the jacket pocket, my heart rate increasing. Mercifully, she looks at it only briefly and hands it back.

'I didn't see the accident,' she tells me. 'I was in bed when it happened. I heard the helicopter when they took him away, but I was... very tired, you know? Wiped out. Later there were some police asking questions but they soon left.'

'Did you know the guy – Professor Visser?'

'I met him at this symposium for the first time. I know of him professionally. I know his – ideas.'

It sounds like whatever his 'ideas' are, she doesn't agree with them, and this snags my interest, but I put it to one side.

'How did it happen? What was he doing?'

'I didn't witness it. You might be better off talking to the hotel staff. But, please, we don't want a simple, unfortunate accident to overshadow the conference. There's so much more important information to be shared and imparted.' Her eyes stray to the doorway through which all this sharing and imparting is going on. 'So, if you'll excuse me.' At least she smiles before ditching out on me. 'Nice to meet you. And, please, look around. You might learn something new.'

She waves an arm at the room before returning the iPad to the desk. At the rope barrier she has a quiet word with the security guy and his eyes move in my direction. Then she passes into the inner sanctum, mingling with the people gathered there.

So that's Laura's love rival. I have put a name to her and noted that she seems smart, cute and committed. I kind of liked her. Until she blew cold at the end, there was something spiky and fun about her. But I don't know how much of what she said was professional ass-covering, and I appear to have trashed my chances of getting past the conference barrier. But I'm not ready to leave yet.

Eighteen

I linger in the public lobby viewing other exhibits that highlight the various factors involved in the ecological disaster that is already happening. There are wall charts of fossil fuel statistics, coloured pie charts accompanied by arty but shocking photographs of haze from industrial pollution in urban China and smoke from forest burning in rural Sumatra. Maps and satellite images show the extent of deforestation in Brazil, along with photos of vast herds of white long-horned beef cattle grazing on the stripped acres. Interactive screens illustrate the periodic depletion of coral reefs and populations of various species of sea life. On other screens, massive icebergs – sudden tons of ice displaced from cliff faces not, allegedly, by time but by global warming – are shown calving into the ocean.

It is all spectacular but depressing stuff that I've never given much thought to until now. Well, a couple of thoughts, anyway. One is, we're all fucked. And the other is, what can *I* do about it? I don't even have the choice to boycott bottled water since the tap water where I live isn't safe to drink.

Someone has left a stray copy of the conference programme on a table and I pick it up and start leafing through it. I learn that ASEAN stands for Association of South East Asian Nations and that our little island is a part of it. I guess it's something like the European Union. Which makes us equivalent to, say, Ibiza.

The schedule of conference events is a list of bewildering presentation titles, each as long as a sentence, peppered with terms like 'thermal oxidizers', 'groundwater recharge', 'radiative forcing', 'ferrofluid', 'polymer degradation' and – one that I can at least break down into words – 'sixth mass extinction event'. The presentations are spread over four 'chambers', each with its own name, plus the large hall at the far end of the building, where the main papers by the top bods are being delivered.

I scan through the names of the speakers, each accompanied by a glossy mugshot and a list of credentials, and don't recognise a single one of them, least of all Laura Duxton because she isn't there. A quick inspection shows that Laura's name isn't mentioned in the full list of delegates in the back pages either, nor anywhere else in the entire programme. I glance around and slip it into my satchel while no one is looking. Damn, I wish I could get past that barrier, just to see if Laura really is in there or not.

Suppose she isn't a delegate. Why else might she be here? One answer to that question has already occurred to me. I wander over to the desk and flash my phoney press pass at the young ponytailed woman that Kristina spoke with.

'Hi. Could you do me a favour and see if there's a journalist on the press list named Laura Duxton?'

She smiles, reassured by the *Straits Times* logo, and checks the iPad for me.

'Sorry. No one with that name here.'

I'm about to turn away when another thought hits me.

'I'm writing a story about Professor Visser's accident yesterday. Is it possible for me to see where he fell from?'

'I'll find someone to help you. Just one moment, please.' She picks up the desk phone and speaks in the local language, then hangs up with a trained smile. 'Someone will be here shortly.'

I wait by the desk, praying that my fake pass and my bogus reporter act both hold up to scrutiny. After a minute or two, a tall, suave man of about my age with a slick hairstyle and a smart suit joins me and shakes my hand but holds back on the friendly face.

'Hello. I'm Mr Lau, the assistant manager of Shiri Palace.'

My heart is thumping as I say, 'Bob Lorrimer, *Straits Times*.' I hold up the pass with my photo on it next to my face. Look, it's me. He glances at it, doesn't question it,

Before the Gulf

actually believes it, and both of us relax while I put it back in my pocket.

'I understand you want to report the accident,' says Mr Lau. 'Isn't it a little late for that?'

I get the feeling that he isn't being sarcastic.

'I'm not reporting it, sir, I'm writing a follow-up piece. A feature. On Professor Visser.'

'Ah, yes! Professor Visser!' Mr Lau smiles at the professor's name as if they are old chums, and his demeanour relaxes a good deal more. Then his face turns serious with concern. 'Such a terrible accident. I'm so glad he survived. I hear he should make a full recovery. The fall, fortunately, was not so far.'

I give Mr Lau the sincerest look I can muster. 'Mr Lau, could you show me where the accident took place? It would very much help me with the background for my article.'

He looks unsure so I sweeten the pill:

'I'd like to be able to tell my readers that Shiri Palace is a safe place and in no way to blame for what happened.'

Mr Lau contemplates this for a moment, no doubt weighing up the cost of liability if Visser was to sue. An endorsement of the Palace's safety standards from the *Straits Times* might be a big feather to impress his bosses with. Finally, he turns to the receptionist.

'Mina, key to room two-two-seven, please.'

She hands him a key-card with the same textbook smile and he leads me towards the elevators.

On the way up to the second floor, Mr Lau explains that Professor Visser's room has been left unoccupied in case he is able to return within the duration of his reservation, but after the police finished their inspections it was cleaned and tidied. We march in step down a long, plush, new-smelling corridor to room 227.

Inside, the bedroom is dominated by a king-size bed, something I haven't seen nor had the pleasure of stretching out on in a very long time. I try not to let my envy show. Facing the bed is a flat-screen television the size of a school

77

blackboard. I don't bother looking in the *en suite*. Two of the professor's shirts and a pair of his trousers are hanging up in the wardrobe. His zipped-up suitcase is still there on the riser. No other obvious possessions of his, nothing by the bed. I guess they'll have transported his personal effects with him to the hospital.

'Do you mind if I…?'

I move towards the French windows that open onto the balcony and Mr Lau obligingly unlatches them for me. The balcony, which overlooks a large inner courtyard with a swimming pool, is made of solid stone underfoot. There's no sign of any loose masonry or anything like that. Everything looks as solid and reliable as the day it was built. An ornamental wrought-iron barrier rail rises to well above my hips. You'd have to climb over it or lean out beyond your tipping point in order to fall accidentally from here. Although I guess the Dutch can be very tall: his tipping point might be different to mine. The drop to the poolside paving below looks about twenty feet. Ouch.

'Is that where he fell?' I say, pointing to the blue slabs directly below.

'Yes, but slightly to the right.'

A few feet further out and he'd have landed on a sun-lounger. Or a sun-bather.

'Was anyone by the pool when it happened?'

'No. No one saw him fall. We only guess he fell from here because this is his room, and he was dressed in his bathrobe. But I think if he fell from a higher floor, he would not be alive.'

The slabs below are spotless.

'You cleaned the blood up?'

'Not much blood. Only a little, here…' Mr Lau touches his forehead. 'But broken bones, plenty.'

I turn back into the room and Mr Lau closes the windows.

'Everything looks completely safe. Whatever Professor Visser was doing, it looks like a clear case of misadventure. Have you spoken to the professor since the accident?'

'Not I. But some of his colleagues have. They say he is very damaged but awake and able to talk. He says he doesn't remember what happened.'

I try to think of questions a reporter would ask. Making them up is beginning to tire me and I wish that Mr Lau would leave me alone to my own devices but I doubt that's going to happen.

'Earlier, you smiled as if you knew him. *Do* you know him?'

'Only from the night shift. Sometimes he is... last from the bar, you know? I was on duty for two nights when we chatted. He's a nice man, very interested in local climate and culture. Interesting to talk to. And he makes good jokes. A good companion.'

And a good tipper, I think cynically.

'Do you think he was alone when he fell? Was anyone else in the room?'

'Not to my knowledge.'

'Did the police find signs that anyone else had been in here? Another guest, perhaps. Or... a friend? A companion?'

Mr Lau doesn't need it spelling out that I'm talking about prostitutes and other sexual partners.

'No. Nothing like that. And please, you must not print any such speculation. When he left the bar and went to bed, Professor Visser was quite alone.'

'No, of course not, absolutely. I'm just wondering if the police found any evidence at all that he might have been... pushed.'

'The police didn't look for any such evidence so they cannot suspect it. The police are satisfied that it was an accident, and that if it was anyone's fault it was the professor's. Clear safety regulations are posted in all our rooms in English.' Mr Lau points to a notice on the back of the door. 'And Professor Visser left the bar very late the night before. I'm sorry to say this because he is a very kind and respectful gentleman and I wish him a full recovery.'

The implication being that he was pie-eyed when he finally crashed out and whatever happened was the fault of his own indulgence.

That feels like an interview closer. I thank Mr Lau for his time and he takes me back down to the lobby and shakes my hand again before leaving me by the front desk. I look toward the conference area, itching to go in but with little hope of getting past the bouncers and no inclination to try.

I'm about to leave when the side doors in the conference area open on the hour as speeches end and the delegates pour out, many sauntering through to the public lobby. Laura isn't visible among them, but someone else is, and heading in my direction.

'Mr Lorrimer,' says Kristina.

No longer Bob, I note – the familiarity reined in for the benefit of the man beside her, perhaps. Kristina's lover. Laura's ex.

Nineteen

'You're still here,' she says. 'Did you get your story?'

'Some of it.'

'What's this?' the man interrupts genially.

'Let me introduce you,' says Kristina. 'Doctor Nicholas Davenport, one of the keynote speakers. And this is Robert Lorrimer of the *Singapore Straits Times*.'

We shake hands and he does that crushing thing that only alpha males or maybe Freemasons do. I guess he thinks he's being manly but it makes a lousy first impression.

'So what's this story you're after?' he asks me.

'Pieter Visser.' I deliberately don't mention the accident, just the name.

'Ah, Pieter!' For the second time, the professor's name elicits a mirthful reaction. 'There's very little story there, I'm afraid. Decent chap, glad he's on the mend and all that, but not a person of any great consequence to someone like you, I wouldn't have thought.'

I'm getting tired of people telling me what I am like.

'Know him well, do you?' I ask him.

'We've met. Appeared on the same bill a few times, as it were.'

'Only, I heard he likes a taste.'

'A what?'

'A drink. Which may account for his fall from the balcony.'

Davenport narrows his eyes at me.

'Look, Mr – '

'Bob... please.'

'Look, Bob.' He puts a hand on my shoulder and turns me aside from Kristina. 'I don't want to be quoted on this, so it's off the record, all right?'

I nod. 'Go on.'

'Pieter Visser has had it rough over the last year or two. Academically speaking. Some of his ideas, his methods, have been called into question. And, yes, he drinks, and maybe some of us could see it coming to a head at this conference. But the poor man has suffered enough now and perhaps we should all cut him a little slack.'

It is a pretty damning speech for someone talking off the record, and I take it with a pinch of salt. If Davenport can rubbish Pieter Visser like this yet insist on deniability, I can easily see how he would two-time Laura with someone like Kristina. This guy has done no wrong to me and I still don't like him one bit. Luckily for me, unluckily for him, we were never on any kind of record in the first place so I owe him no confidentiality. I think about slapping down the name Laura Duxton, but don't know what it will achieve other than to show my hand.

'You'd be better off writing about what's going on in there.' Davenport indicates the conference hall.

'My colleague Gail Riviera is covering it,' I say archly, dropping her memorable name for my own credibility. 'But just out of interest, what is going on in there?'

'Oh, just a bunch of tech wizards trying to save the world.'

And trying to auction their inventions to the highest bidder, I think cynically, glancing at the throng of smart suits and power frocks.

After a couple of two-faced pleasantries I thank him and Kristina for their time and wish them good luck and they wander back into the conference.

I can't think of any reason to hang around. I walk out the door and the heat of the sun climbing towards noon hits me full on. I tread down the slip road to where the bike is parked, but instead of turning back north towards home I continue south to follow the road all the way round to the island capital on the west coast, to the hospital where they took Pieter Visser.

Twenty

I stop off at a liquor store in the town and buy a half bottle of vodka, then stow it in my satchel. By the time I reach the hospital, thunderhead clouds are threatening another heavy afternoon shower. I park the bike in a covered area and find my way to reception. When I ask for Pieter Visser who was brought in by helicopter yesterday, the nurse behind the desk directs me to a private room along a corridor on the ground floor. I tap lightly on the door before poking my head around it.

'Professor Visser?'

The room is pink-walled and fresh-smelling. The man under powder-blue sheets on the bed has one arm in a plaster cast, supported in the air at an angle by a structure of interlocking metal rods. His other arm is cradled in a sling across his chest. A bandage is wound around his skull in such a way as to cover the forehead injury Mr Lau described to me. A healthy mop of brown hair sticks out of the top like weeds in broken concrete. There seem to be other bandages around his ribcage.

He is awake. When he slowly turns his head away from the window and I look him in the eye I notice how bruised his face is, both eyes blackened and plum-coloured all around them. His body is attached to a drip and a monitor but there is no oxygen tube or mask. Underneath the damage is an otherwise rangy-looking avuncular middle-aged man whose well-fed good looks it takes only a little imagination to see.

'Yes?' he groans in a deep, drowsy voice.

'May I come in?'

He tries to shift in the bed, mustering his strength.

'Are you a doctor? You don't look like a doctor.'

His accent, though slight, is unmistakably Dutch, like talking and swallowing at the same time.

83

'No, I'm not a doctor. Just a visitor.' By now I'm in the door and nudging it shut behind me. 'My name's Bob, sir. Bob Lorrimer.'

'And what do you want, Bob Lorrimer?'

'I wanted to talk to you about this weekend's conference. And about your accident.'

'Oh, you're a reporter. Do me a favour, Bob. Pass me some water.'

Everybody hates reporters in the movies but I seem to be doing all right at it. With Mr Lau I put it down to the natural friendliness and lack of suspicion in the Southeast Asian temperament. Perhaps the same goes for the Dutch. Or perhaps Pieter Visser has a story of his own that he wants to tell.

I move to his bedside. On the trolley is a jug of water and one of those plastic mugs with a spout that small children use. I half fill the mug, hold it to his lips and tip it gently. His eyes flash when he's sipped enough. I replace the mug and notice the sky darkening and a wind in the trees outside the window.

'Thank you, Bob.'

'They're still keeping your room reserved for you at Shiri Palace,' I say.

'Well, if you go back there, tell them it's very kind of them, but I don't think I'll be returning within the remaining time frame. I think I might be here for quite a bit longer than that. But don't worry, Bob. The university will take care of me.'

'University of Utrecht. Professor of... Earth and Environment?'

'Professor is just a fancy made-up title that anyone can call themselves. I don't like it. It's pretentious. But everyone calls me Professor, I don't know why. It reminds me of Felix the Cat.'

He goes off at this point into an impressively high-pitched squeak: 'It's the Professor!' The allusion is clearly lost on me, from before my time.

'Officially, I'm the head of my department. If you want my academic title, it's Doctor. I have two doctorates but only the one title. Make sure you get that right when you write your story. Who is it for?'

'Er, the *Singapore Straits Times*.'

I take out the pass and hold it where he can see it.

'You flew from Singapore to interview me?'

I don't want to string him along any more than I have to. 'I'm a local correspondent.'

His eyes twinkle with interest. 'You live here on the island?'

'Yes.'

'Tell me, what is it like here in the monsoon season?'

'Wet. Windy. Dreary. Life moves indoors.'

'Indeed.' He says this as if I've told him something he can't imagine for himself. He seems to drift off into deep thought.

'Pro— Dr Visser?'

'Sorry. The drugs make me tired. Sometimes I "zone out"' – saying it like a new phrase he's recently picked up.

I realise that my ploy of loosening his tongue with the vodka might not be wise.

'I can come back another time,' I say diplomatically.

The first enfilade of rain crashes against the window and thunder explodes over the hills, quickly followed by a lightning flash. Now is not the best time to have to leave, and I hope he's zoned in enough to pick up on this.

'No. Please. Sit down. Ask me your questions.'

I pull up a chair and take out my notebook and pen to look more like a journalist; though nowadays a real journalist, I know from films and TV, would bring out some kind of recording device at this point. I push on and jump in with the obvious.

'What happened?'

'Hah—' Visser's involuntary attempt at laughter turns to a brief coughing fit that he soon gets under control. 'Fuck!

That hurts! Sorry. I'm laughing at your question because I can't remember. I don't know!'
'Were you awake before it happened?'
'Yes. I'm sure I was. I went to bed very late. They will keep the bar there open for you until whatever time you decide to go to bed, and since I was free to sleep till noon if I wished, I... made the most of the hospitality, shall we say? But about ten-thirty the sunshine in the room woke me up.'
I watch him replay it frame by frame in his head.
'I felt groggy. I needed more sleep but it was too bright. So I got out of bed and put on a robe and went to close the drapes.' His eyes shrink, peering into the past as if it were much longer than just twenty-five hours ago. 'I remember the doors to the balcony were open. I must have left them open when I went to bed. And I stepped out to look at the morning. I yawned. I stretched...'
His eyes return to me.
'After that I was waking up in this place.'
'Did you lean against the railing?'
His eyes flick back to the past. 'Ye-es... I stepped to the front of the balcony... and leaned out a little, to look left and right. I remember the pool was empty, as if everyone else was still asleep also.'
'And then?'
'And then, nothing. Ka-put!'
'Could you have slipped?'
'No. My feet were naked and would not slip on that surface.'
'Was the floor wet, maybe?'
'No. There had been no prior precipitation.'
'Sorry?'
'It hadn't rained recently. Not since I arrived.' He tilts his head towards the window. 'This is the first rain I've seen here. Though they tell me it rained yesterday, while the surgeons were setting my bones.'

His interest in the weather pattern is presumably stoked by professional concerns. 'It's usual for this time of year,' I tell him.

'How long have you been here?'

'Five years. Going back to the accident, do you think you could have leaned out too far without realising?'

'I can control the geometry of my own body without thinking about it, as can everyone else.' He notices my puzzled expression. 'I know when I'm leaning out too far.'

'But you said, yourself, you were groggy.'

'I might have been groggy but I wasn't stupid.'

Something in Visser's demeanour has set as rigid as the cast on his broken arm. Caution against liability? Further loss of professional regard? Unwillingness to admit to a drink problem? It could be any or all of those things. But it was just an avenue I wanted to close off anyway before my next question.

'Dr Visser. May I ask – was anyone else in your room with you that morning?'

He seems surprised by the question. 'No. I went to bed alone. I came to the conference alone.'

Simple facts. No trace of self-pity. He's accustomed to being alone, like me.

'Could anyone have come into the room while you were out on the balcony?'

'I think I would have heard them. The maid always knocks first.'

'But if someone had a key-card. Let themselves in quietly.'

'Mr Lorrimer, you sound more like a police person now than a reporter. You think someone might have pushed me?'

'Is it possible?'

He thinks carefully, perhaps even statistically. 'It's possible. But I have no memory of anyone entering the room or anyone pushing me.'

Facts again. For the record. I think about my next question.

'Can you think of anyone who might wish you harm?'
He coughs again and I wonder if I've gone too far but the cough turns to a laugh this time.
'After the party the night before, I can think of a few. But seriously? No. Even they wouldn't go that far.'
'Who's they?'
'Too many to mention.'
I don't want this turning into an Agatha Christie mystery. I'm about to throw some names at him to narrow it down but he's still busy coughing, and swearing in Dutch.
A nurse comes into the room and smiles at me. She leans over him to adjust the pillow supporting his neck.
'Professor very tired. Needs rest.'
The message is clear and my heart sinks for a moment because I still don't have any helpful answers. Then Visser stops coughing.
'Aargh, that hurts. I'm tired now, Bob. Can you come back tomorrow? There's more you should know.'
'Of course. Of course.' I look at the nurse over by the monitor and she nods her approval. 'I'll leave you to get some rest. And thanks for your time.'
The thunder and lightning passed over quickly and the rain won't go on much longer. I sit in a waiting room until the shower ends, writing up my notes on this morning's enquiries.
Visser is right, I do sound like a detective. But if there is a crime at all, I've yet to find it. I've pretty much established that Laura lied to me about being a speaker at the conference. And I've learned that humanity is on the brink of extinction. Apart from that, nothing; certainly nothing criminal. Other than on a global economic scale, of course.
I wind back and remind myself that it was never about that. It's about finding out who Laura Duxton really is, and why she has suddenly cropped up in my life. And with that thought, an uncomfortable truth drives a little closer to home.
It is about me.

Twenty-one

I've tried to keep my story in the present and moving forward, but inevitably it has drawn me back to the past, the pull of which will not be resisted any more. The backstory of me. Or some of it, for now.

I arrived on the island five years ago. You already know that because I said so earlier. But I didn't arrive in the usual way, by air. You already know that too. When I said I 'washed up' here, I meant it pretty much literally. I arrived as the sole passenger on a small Indonesian trading vessel. I worked hard for my passage as a stevedore, loading and unloading at various ports on the voyage from Bali, which was not long, no more than a fortnight.

For three years before that I'd bummed around Southeast Asia on my own, the last two of those avoiding big tourist destinations to follow less beaten tracks. The backpacker trail that I'd followed for the first year I quickly abandoned when a British guy freaked me out by saying he thought he'd seen me somewhere before, maybe on TV. I was working in a bar on Kuta Beach at the time. After that I worked on farms in Vietnam, slept in seedy backstreet hostels in Malacca and lodged with Buddhist monks in Chiang Mai, and I can tell you that there are snakes that live in inundated rice paddies, the industrial west coast of Malaysia is not pretty, and the hill forests of the Karen territory are the worst for leeches.

At the monastery in Chiang Mai, halfway up the mountain road that leads to the Queen of Thailand's palace, I swept floors most of the day for my board and lodging, occasionally helping in the kitchen. I stayed there four or five months to dodge the rainy season. I wouldn't say it was a quiet existence, there was a lot of chanting and bell ringing, but it was an untroubled one. Routine suited me; it was what I'd once been used to and it was oddly nice to get back to it.

But other than reading and some music on an old Walkman there wasn't a great deal at first to occupy my mind. I was expected to kneel with the monks and make the required gestures at prayer time but whatever they were chanting was in a foreign language and of no sense or interest to me. I just went through the motions to be polite and for the sake of my supper.

Almost from the get go, certain monks would sit and spend time with me in the hottest part of the day when we rested from our labour because I was a resource for them to practise their English with. I didn't mind: they did it quite openly with all the western guests who passed through, and it was another way I could be of use, not a nuisance. But because I stayed there a long time, and as the demands of their conversations became more challenging, I started to feel like a useful member of the human race for the first time in my life; I had taken on the role of a teacher. The experience taught me a lot about my own language, about how to analyse it and how to use it clearly and effectively. And it was there, during that time, that I conceived the idea of becoming a writer in exile.

As my discussions with the monks deepened, they explained to me the central ideas of Buddhism and the meanings of the daily prayers and rituals. Buddhism, I concluded, isn't a religion at all, at least not by the standards of any of the others. It has no godhead. Buddha was a person, like Jesus, but born of nature, of real people, without any divine intervention; he was just a man. Well, a prince. And all he asked was that we be nice to each other and to all living things. It was interesting, thought-provoking and persuasive stuff and it made me more aware of what the daily services were for, which in turn made the long days go more pleasantly.

My time at the monastery taught me a lot. It taught me how to slow down, alter my pace of life, modify my expectations of other people and ignore the demands of any meaningless agenda. It taught me how to listen to others without arguing back at them. It taught me how to judge what is and what isn't important, and to let the unimportant go. It taught me about the versatility of English, showed me the complex beauty of language and made me want to be a writer. And it taught me a hell of a lot about how to sweep floors.

But what I never learned from the monks before I left the monastery was Buddha's position on forgiveness. To be fair, I never asked them. If I had, I'm sure they would have loved the opportunity to explain it to me. But I couldn't make myself do it. I couldn't bring myself to ask them. My head was still too full of chaplain rhetoric about guilt, forgiveness's progenitor. It always felt like a discussion I couldn't face. So I never did.

As my time there drew on, I became clearer in my mind. I don't mean clarity of thinking, I mean clearance of thoughts. Mindfulness. To ask them my question before I departed would have been to ask for a parting pearl of wisdom that I no longer felt I needed, because I had learned to let it go. It would have been too corny. So I didn't. And it was another two years before I got the chance again.

Then one day, I'm sitting in a Bob Marley bar drinking bottles of Singha or Tiger with Panda – this was not long after I bought my first bike, a second-hand Yamaha – and he says as part of some bullshit conversation we're having:

'I was a priest once. Went to priest school for two years.'

It did and didn't surprise me. It made me laugh, but I had already begun to notice his Buddha-like attributes, and knew that it was common for young men here to give it a go, like a kind of voluntary national service. I asked him then about the Buddhist attitude towards forgiveness, and he told me. Explained it all to me at great length. And the next morning I woke up and I had forgotten all of it because I'd been too drunk to take any of it in. So later that day I visited Panda at his place, and in private I found myself confessing to him what I had done.

Panda told me that the kind of forgiveness I was talking about was irrelevant. It wasn't about striving for the forgiveness of another party, it was about striving for the forgiveness of the cosmos. This is achieved by living the best life you can live, over and over if necessary, until you reach nirvana, the perfect peace. Other people's forgiveness is a part of their own journey. And if the road to nirvana means letting go of earthly possessions, it also means letting go of guilt.

'You gotta do it, brother. You gotta find a way.'

And I was getting along nicely pretending that I had.

Until now.

Twenty-two

From the hospital it takes me about an hour to ride home back along the southern coast, the way I came. At the hut I change into T-shirt and shorts, then carefully fold all the new clothes and stow them, along with the moccasins, in my suitcase under the bed. I count what's left of my cash and thank my lucky stars that Mr Lau valued his position at Shiri Palace too much to risk eliciting a bribe from a reporter. I still have about eighty dollars' worth of local currency but I intend to spend it as parsimoniously as I can.

I start by going out for the least expensive lunch I can find. Then I spend a couple of hours loafing around Danny's bar, trying to read the book Laura gave me, but distracted by all that I've discovered in the last few days.

There could be a perfectly sound reason why I saw no trace of Laura's name in the conference literature. She might have been a last-minute replacement for someone who had to drop out, and the programme may have already gone to the printers before her name could be added. But if she isn't a participant in the conference, then maybe she's here stalking Nick Davenport, her unfaithful ex. Maybe her agenda is entirely personal and nothing to do with science or the environment – or me.

That's one theory. It would explain why she's lied about herself: she doesn't want to come across as a 'psycho bitch from hell'. It might also account for inconsistencies in the story she's fabricated for herself. For instance, she said that staying in the beach hut instead of Shiri Palace would save money for her *department*, from which I inferred that she worked in a university. But later she said she worked for some tech giant. There could be any number of reasons why she said 'department', not 'company'. Maybe she works for both. But it's just one mismatch among a few that I've noticed.

Another theory is that she's lying low from her complicity in Pieter Visser's 'accident'. That would explain her wanting to keep her distance from Shiri Palace and to be seen to be staying elsewhere; and maybe even her apparent absence today from the conference. But nothing in Visser's account suggests that anyone pushed him, an idea he would surely have been open to if he thought there could be any truth in it, but he was not. And why would Laura associate herself with the conference at all if her object in general was to dissociate herself from it in order to carry out some covert assassination attempt? This theory makes no sense yet. But it's an avenue I won't abandon until I find out who was at that party in the bar that night.

It isn't impossible that Laura was there herself. I don't know what she did after I left her to go to work the night she arrived, only that she was still up and out on her porch when I got back after four. It's possible that she hadn't long since returned. She could have been up at Shiri Palace until three, three-thirty easy, and I'd have had no way of knowing.

A third theory nagging at the back of my brain is that she is somehow here for me. Perhaps egoism is the only basis for this; a vague wish on my part for a happy fate bringing a sympathetic woman into my life. The handful of hours that I've spent in her company can be accounted for by normal happenstance, and relations between us have been predominantly pragmatic, and never anything beyond platonic. Even the kiss she gave me on the cheek can be interpreted as no more than a show of gratitude for the help of a friendly stranger in a strange land.

But then I think back to that brief but unmistakable fear in her eyes when I surprised her on the porch in the rain the other day, and I wonder if there could be some truth to this third theory beyond ego. What if I'm the one being stalked? She could be anyone. She could know who I am. She could know what I've done…

With all these questions going round in my head, the mystery of Laura deepens until I realise I've been sitting for a long time simply gazing at a mental picture of her, like the lovesick teenager that Lily took me for.

I return my attention to *The Quiet American*, and quickly learn that the first-person narrator is an Englishman abroad called Fowler, and a journalist. Perhaps he is someone I can learn some pointers from if I'm going to continue my private masquerade as Bob Lorrimer. I certainly intend to revisit Visser in hospital tomorrow, ask him more about that party in the bar and see where that leads me. I've kept Laura's name as a card up my sleeve so far; maybe tomorrow I'll put it into play.

The setting of the book is Southeast Asia. Fowler is not alone, he has a Vietnamese lover, Phuong. But Pyle, the third party in what seems destined to be a love triangle, is the most interesting character. Like Laura, Pyle is a foreign interloper with a secret agenda. As I read, I fixate more and more on this parallel. Did Laura give me this to read out of some other reason than goodwill? I let my imagination run riot again, looking through the words on the page to a possible deeper meaning. It's as if she has handed me a coded guide book to whatever the fuck is going on. But when I focus on the text, any message, any clue, soon becomes lost down the different road of Greene's own story. It's just a fanciful notion and I let it go.

I don't know if Greene is a better writer than Hemingway because I've never actually read any Hemingway. The stuff about 'one true sentence' I picked up from a magazine article, and just always remembered it, in case I ever became a writer one day. But Greene's prose is very good. The characters and setting are drawn with telling particularities, not a word wasted, and the plot is skilfully constructed. You feel that Greene must be Fowler, must have lived through this story to write it so authentically. Suddenly, I feel downhearted. I'll never write anything as good as this. I would need to have been honing my craft through all those years when I had the chance but failed to take it.

I put the book down with the realisation that all I'm doing is killing time until Laura returns from the conference, or wherever it is she otherwise went to ground. So I pack up my stuff, finish my Fanta, visit the loo on my way out, then head back to Lily's to wait for her, seething with unconfirmed suspicions like some jealous husband.

Twenty-three

It grows dark and Laura hasn't yet returned to her hut. I decide I'm not going to work tonight, fuck it, everyone deserves a weekend off every now and then. Once the decision is made, I crack open a bottle of rum I've been keeping aside for ages, a gift from a nice Swedish man who once hired me for a week to take him round all the island's prominent sights. I light a mosquito coil and sit out on the porch, looking at the stars.

I'm reminded of one night from my childhood when Cory Stewart and I were out stargazing in his parents' front garden with Cory's telescope. It was nothing fancy, just a white tube about a foot and a half long with an extendable eyepiece. It had a short detachable tripod but we mostly looked through it holding it in our hands, pirate fashion. Really it was just an expensive child's toy. I don't know how we started to argue over it. Arguing was something that often happened with Cory, and he was older and bigger than me. All I remember next is that it ended with Cory batting the fat end of the telescope with his hand while I was looking through it, and Mum and Dad having to take me to hospital with what they thought might be a fractured eye socket but which turned out to be nothing worse than a black eye. Of course, Cory told everyone it was an accident, and they would all rather believe him and make me stand there and accept his phoney apology than have to think the worst of him. Because that would have upset all the apples...

I push the memory back in its box and take a swig of the sweet-tasting rum and follow a line of stars to a constellation I can actually recognise and name. After a while, a small offshoot flock of fruit bats descends on the trees in Lily's orchard, and I let the sound of the crickets and the breakers and the smell of the tropical night soothe my troubled thoughts.

Stress can have a funny habit of making people feel sleepy (I'm sure the rum had nothing to do with it!) and by the time Laura gets back I have fallen into a light snooze. Her 'hello' wakes me up and I stir gently, unprepared for what to say to her, all my rehearsed recriminations suddenly deflated.

'Hi.'

'Not working tonight?'

'Thought I'd take the weekend off. How'd it go?'

She's shouldering a laptop bag. 'Let me get rid of this.'

She disappears into her hut and returns five minutes later changed into slacks and a long-sleeved T-shirt against the mosquitoes. She's clutching a small can of insect repellent, which she sprays around her bare ankles.

'Want some of this?'

'I'm fine,' I say.

'Are you one of these people they don't bite?'

'I wish I was. But they're all-year-round here, and I don't wanna put nasty chemicals on my skin every day, so you just get used to them. So… *how'd it go today?*'

'*Is that rum?*'

Our questions overlap and we both laugh, me wondering whether it was deliberate deflection of my persistent question on her part.

'Yeah, it is,' I say into the confusion.'Do you want some? I can fetch you a glass.'

'Yes, please, that'd be lovely.'

'I don't have any mixers. Only bottled water.'

'Oh, no, straight, please. You don't want to spoil good rum with any nonsense.'

I take two glasses off the shelf in the bathroom, give them a rinse and a wipe and bring them outside and pour two fingers of the rum into one for her and two in the other glass for me. We clink glasses and I try a third time:

'So how'd it go?'

'It went fine. I think it was well-received.'

'By your colleagues.'

'That's right.'

'I wish I could've been there.'

'Oh, it was just a lot of boring technical stuff. You know.'

'No, I don't. Why don't you give me a summary?'

I'm being pushy. She looks me queerly in the eye, either thinking to herself 'what's going on here?' or stalling for time, I can't decide which.

'Well... it's about microplastics. You know what those are?'

'Tiny indestructible particles of plastic floating in the ocean.'

'Not just in the ocean. In the ground, in our rivers, in the very air that we breathe and in the food that we eat. They're in *us*, you and me, right now. We inhale them from the synthetic clothes that we wear and the soft furnishings that we fill our homes with. We consume them second-hand from animals inside the meat and fish that we eat. If you drink bottled water, you consume ninety thousand more particles a year than if you drink tap water. If bottles get reused or stand in the shop too long, the plastic leaches into the water and that number increases. So they can't be safely recycled for purpose.'

'And if you drink the tap water here, you get bilharzia. I know which I'd rather *not* have.'

'I know. And that's one of the problems ASEAN has to address. The provision of potable water supplies.'

'Is that what your talk was about?'

'In a way.' She pauses, looks away, then turns back to me. 'There are new methods being devised to gather and remove microplastics from rivers and outflows before they reach the ocean. The problem is, they work in small-scale demonstrations in the lab but someone has to develop the technology to make them work on an industrial scale that can be applied globally.'

She's hitting all the right buzzwords.

'And that someone is you,' I say. 'But wasn't it all things "industrial" that got us into this mess in the first place?'

'Well, yes, but... what's the alternative? Ignore it and hope it'll go away?'

'But it doesn't go away, does it? You just move it from one place to another.'

'Now that's where you're wrong. Plastic may, to all practical considerations, be non-biodegradable but it isn't actually indestructible. It can be dissolved in acetone. And it can be converted into fuel, either by pyrolysis or incinerators that generate electricity.'

She is losing me now with words like 'pyrowhatsit', and I respond characteristically. 'Is electricity a fuel?'

'You know what I mean, smart arse.'

I sip my rum and give her an appraising look while her head is down laughing gently. She could be shitting me, but it all sounds convincing. Maybe I'm wrong about her. Maybe I'm making it all up. I expected this conversation to lead us into conflict but everything so far suggests a rational explanation well within the acceptable parameters of my conspiracy theories. Of course, I could cross-question her. I could ask her if she was a last-minute replacement speaker, ask her why her name isn't on the programme. But that would give the game away that I've been snooping on her. I have to remind myself that whoever Laura really is, and whatever she is doing here, is technically none of my business. Unless it involves me personally. And if it does, and I blow it now by showing my hand and scaring her away, I'll never find out who she is or what she wants.

'So is that what this conference is all about?' I say, taking a different tack. 'Selling new technology to big corporations?'

'Well someone has to fund it, Mike, and it ain't cheap. Besides, isn't that what we all want? Them to clean up their own mess?'

I wait for a 'but'. I expect her to go on to say that it isn't *all* about that; that it's also about education and responsibility and all that other comforting bullshit that we like to think will make a difference. But she doesn't. So I change tack again.

'Did you see your ex? Did he come to your talk?'

'No. He went to another one. Deliberately, I suspect.'

'Were you disappointed?'

'God, no! I spent the rest of the day avoiding him, and his groupie.'

And me, if only she'd known it. The guy from the beach hut next door. Her own private stalker. What have I been thinking? There's only one way I can put my suspicions about Laura to bed, and I ask her the question as if it's something I've forgotten, although I know she never told me it in the first place.

'What's his name again?'

'Why do you ask?'

'Well, he keeps cropping up in conversation.'

I wait.

'Nick.' She giggles at the sound of it on her tongue. 'Old Nick.'

Right answer. I sip the rum and feel the rhythm of my heart settle down, and change tack again, this time for the home stretch.

'What are you doing for dinner?' I ask her.

Twenty-four

We go Dutch at a fancy tourist place on the strip. We stroll out to a quieter stretch, away from the super-clubs, and pick one where the background music stays in the background and the clientèle don't look like they're getting ready to dance on the tables or start a bar fight. We share a bottle of white wine and I order beef in black bean sauce and she orders prawns with noodles.

'I've been lucky with the food so far,' she says, 'touch wood,' and she taps her hand on the edge of the table.

'It's like the mosquitoes. You get used to it.'

'It's nice here.'

'Yeah. But there's a reason even the locals who can afford it don't eat in tourist places.'

'Jesus. Couldn't you have told me that earlier?'

'Sorry. I'm sure the food's fine here.'

None of this puts her off eating, and my beef tastes fine and isn't inordinately chewy, even though it probably came from a water buffalo. At some point we get to talking about films we've seen and books we've read, normal conversational stuff that is no longer me surreptitiously grilling her about my theories and my paranoia, and as the meal and the wine and the talk progress, I feel myself letting those things go.

Afterwards we walk back slowly and she links her arm through mine and I wave at the occasional passing hoots from moped riders who know me from working the strip. None of them has seen me with a woman before. The gossip will get around – 'Hey, saw Mike last night with a lady friend' – but tonight I don't care.

'What now?' says Laura.

'I thought you had another early start at Shiri Palace tomorrow.'

'I do. But it's still early, isn't it?'

I check the time on my wrist. 'It's nearly nine.'

'We could go to Pyrotek again.'

'How about somewhere a little quieter but still on the beach?'

I take her to Danny's bar. The place is only half full, relaxed, and a young guy on the beach nearby is strumming bossa nova tunes on an acoustic guitar while a three-quarter moon sits above the horizon, casting a track of shimmering beam towards us across the water. It couldn't be more perfect if it had been written that way for us.

We take a pair of tall bar stools and I lean towards Danny as he comes over.

'Hey, Mike.'

'Danny, I want you to meet Laura Duxton. Laura, this is Danny.'

Laura flashes me a funny look, like her attention skips a beat, then smiles at Danny.

'Hi, Danny, nice to meet you.'

They shake hands over the bar top and she flashes me a funny look again before continuing.

'So,' she says, not letting go of his hand yet, 'how long have you known Mike?'

Danny looks at me. 'What is it, Mike? Must be five years?'

'That sounds about right,' I say.

Laura releases Danny's hand. 'Mike tells me he came here to write a book. Is that right?'

Danny grins at me. 'I see him sitting there doodling in that pad of his. He never told me he was writing a book.'

'It's just that five years seems like an awfully long time to write – what is it? Three sentences?'

I pretend it's a joke, which I hope it is. 'What can I say? I'm my own worst editor. Or best, depending how you look at it.'

'Anyway,' says Danny, 'nice to meet you, Laura. What can I get you?'

Danny serves us drinks and goes off to be busy elsewhere and I turn to Laura.

'You okay?'

'Yes, fine. Why?'

I can see she doesn't want to talk about those funny looks she gave me, so I deflect the question. 'I mean coming here. Is it okay?'

She gazes around at the moonlit sea and the young guitar player and the other couples enjoying their drinks by candlelight and the warm evening breeze rustling the palms.

'Yes! It's wonderful!'

We move from the bar to a free table and Laura gets to asking me about myself and naturally I think carefully about what to edit out of my backstory.

'What did you do before here?'

I tell her honestly about my prior wanderings, about the backpacker hostels and the bar jobs and the five months in a monastery, obfuscating my conscious decision to hide from western travellers for two years with a non-chronological jumble of impressions.

'Okay,' she says, 'but what about before that? I mean back in Britain.'

'Not much to tell. Left school early, had a number of jobs, got bored, took off abroad. To "find myself".'

'What jobs? Where?'

'Factory jobs, mostly. In the Midlands,' I lie.

'You don't have a Midlands accent. Whereabouts?'

'Nottingham,' I reply, thinking that it's farther north than Birmingham or Wolverhampton and therefore more likely to convincingly fit my actual accent. 'But travelling tends to modify how you speak,' I bullshit. 'You pick up how other travellers speak.'

'Were there any girlfriends along the way?'

'Some,' I say, relieved that her questions have moved away from Britain. 'Nothing that really meant much, or lasted. No marriages or kids. What about you?'

'Ah, we've finished on you, have we? There were boys in school and at university that I fucked.' She looks at me to see if I'm shocked. 'I was an early starter and quite promiscuous. But, no, no one special, until Nick came along.'

'And what was so special about him?'

'He was brilliant, and charismatic. When I took his classes I thought he was a god. We all did, all his students, even the ones who disagreed with his ideas. And, in his field, he *was* a god.'

'Is he still?'

'Well, he's a keynote speaker at conferences all over the world, has dozens of books and hundreds of articles to his name... What do you think?'

'There's something I don't understand. He's this top academic in a university department and you work for a tech firm, but you said that you still work together, in the same place.'

'Yeah,' she drawls. 'It's complicated. Though not that complicated. I teach classes at the university but the research I'm doing is sponsored by a company.'

'So it's commercial research, not pure research?' I say, trying to sound intelligent and still searching for odd angles to her story despite the way she's slotted all the answers squarely into place.

'I guess you could say that.' Her drink is finished and she starts to look restless. 'I suppose I ought to be getting back. Nine o'clock start tomorrow, and all that.'

'More microplastics?'

'Yep.'

'But it's Sunday. It shouldn't be allowed.'

'Environmental degradation doesn't stop for weekends, I'm afraid.'

She puts her arm through mine again on the walk home, and for a while she reaches across herself and rests her free hand on my bicep. Back at the ranch, Lily is out in her rattan chair with her mosquito coil and her cigarette. Seeing Laura

105

on my arm, she squints a dirty look at me on the side, and the two of us wish her a giggly 'good night'.

I walk Laura to the door of her hut and we stand toe to toe on the raised porch.

'Thanks for a lovely evening, Mike.'

She puts a hand up to my face and stands on tiptoes to kiss me on the cheek like before and I turn my head and put my fingers to her chin, guiding her lips onto mine. For a brief moment her eyes close and I keep mine open, then her eyes open again, looking startled into mine, and as she pulls a step away from me it's as if I've glimpsed some ancient and terrible memory buried inside both of us.

'I'm sorry,' I say.

'No. Don't be.' She smiles, apologetically. 'But I need to sleep now.' She brings the palm of her hand back up to my cheek. 'I'll see you tomorrow. Afterwards.'

'It's the last day. Will you be leaving after that?'

'I don't have to. We'll see.'

She turns away into the hut. As I walk back up to mine, I see Lily under her porch light watching me through the trees, shaking her head and muttering something to herself, or perhaps to me. Something nicely sarcastic, like 'Good night... *Mike*.' I go into my hut and shut the door.

Twenty-five

The same damn dream comes back again. Just like Cory. *Cory Stewart's coming back, Cory Stewart's coming back...* I wake up shaking both inside and out. How often does that happen, the exact same dream two nights in a row? Thankfully, this time, it's already morning and I don't have to risk returning to that place; to that face staring at me in my bed.

I reach out of bed to my Timex on the floor and see that it's only nine o'clock. I'm so used to not waking before at least eleven that the time takes me by surprise. Then I recall. After I came into the hut last night I poured myself a stiff rum, reviewed my notes from Shiri Palace and the hospital so that I'd be ready for today, then read some more of *The Quiet American* until the dim light started to do my eyes in. I must've been in bed and asleep by midnight. I've still woken up too late to catch Laura, though, who will be up at the conference again by now.

When I roll out of bed I realise how thick-headed I feel. It's been a long time since I drank so much alcohol and I've turned into a 'lightweight'. The fact is, I hate hangovers so much that, these days, I would rather forgo the pleasure of getting drunk to avoid them. It has to be a special occasion for the sacrifice to be worth it; though I guess my first dinner date in six years *was* a special occasion. Otherwise, just let me coast on my two beers a day. I don't keep any aspirins or anything like that in the hut but my head isn't *too* bad, and a shower and a swim in the sea will soon sort it out.

Afterwards, feeling better, I stroll up to reception but Lily isn't around and everything is locked up. I continue down the side path to the shadowy main strip, which is lightly buzzing with morning traffic and a few tourists, some of whom obviously haven't made it to bed yet. I spot Candy, one of Lily's cronies who runs a small, cramped, cockroach-friendly hostel for budget-conscious backpackers a few doors down from us.

'Hey, Mike,' she calls to me in a voice almost as distinctively birdlike as Lily's. She doesn't seem to be doing much but standing with hands on hips, watching the world go by.

'Hey, Candy. You seen Lily?'

'She wen' out on business. Say she come back soon, an' to watch out for customers while she gone.'

So much for their being competitors. It's what I love about this place: that spirit of 'you scratch my back, I'll scratch yours'. Not that I know what their business arrangements are, or have ever asked. Candy might be in indentured servitude to Lily and I wouldn't have a clue.

'Oh, here she come now.'

Candy points and I spot Lily over the road, waddling towards us. By the direction she's coming from and the harried expression on her face, I can already guess who she's been off doing 'business' with.

'Fucking Bandura!'

Candy and I hear this above the traffic noise while Lily is still crossing the road. It's not like Lily to swear, at least not in English. As she joins us, she continues in full flow, omitting to dial it down at all.

'That man is a pig! He sit there all day behind his big stupid desk and do nothing except take money, take money.' She mimes the refrain with appropriate clutching hand motions. 'No please, no thank you, just take money, take money. He stiff me real good this time. He no captain. He thief! He pirate!'

I see no advantage in pointing out to her that a pirate can be a captain, and a captain can be a thief. Candy says something to Lily in their own language. In tone, it sounds like 'Hey, keep your fucking voice down, you'll get us all arrested' but I can't attest to that as a direct translation.

'Calm down, Lily,' I say to her, 'deep breaths.' She lights a cigarette. 'What d'you mean, he stiffed you?'

'He raise his cut. Now I have to raise my prices.'

'Why?'

'Cos he a greedy fat pig! Do nothing all day 'cept take money, take money.'

'I mean, why you? Why now?'

'He say my business do too much good. Like he know anything! He say I should pay fifteen percent now until end of season.'

'Then it goes back down to ten?'

'You think so? I don' think so. Once Bandura get money, he hold on to it like a tiger.' Her hand makes a fist. 'He never give it back.'

I try to hide an irresistible smile; she's just described herself. Maybe it's a national characteristic. They do have a lion doing something very similar on their beer bottles.

'No good smiling,' says Lily, smacking my arm. 'He do same for you, too, you see.' She waves a hand at Candy too. 'He raise fifteen percent for everyone. You see.'

'Did he say that?'

'He no say to me, but you see. You ask around. I bet.'

I'm not going to take that bet at any odds. But why? Bandura's cut has been ten percent since... forever. Why is he upping it now? Maybe it indicates 'something in the wind'. On an island like this, there's always talk of something in the wind. It could presage good news or it could be bad but, whatever it is, it will affect us all. I know one thing, though: not even someone as venal as Bandura would jeopardise the tourist industry, the proverbial goose that keeps on giving.

We leave Candy to get on with the rest of her day. Lily serves our breakfast out on the porch to the music of morning birdsong, if only she will shut up about Bandura so we can hear it. She bought a bag of croissants while she was out, so today my luck must be in. Let's hope it holds. Once our mouths are occupied with food, a peaceful calm descends. There's only the birds, the sea and the civilised tinkle of the spoons in our breakfast bowls, set to the *andante* rhythm of a *basso profundo* snore drifting up from one of the huts.

'You fuck that girl?'

It comes out of nowhere, blindsiding me. My face screws up in disbelief.

'*What!?*'

'I see you last night, you two, making kissy-kissy.'

'You sound like Miss Piggy. Don't be daft, you're embarrassing yourself.'

'Daft? What's "daft"?'

'Stupid. Daft means stupid.'

Lily clatters her bowl down on the table and is immediately on her feet, heading my way across a very short distance. I manage to put down my own bowl before raising my arms, or else I'd be nursing a lapful of papaya and banana. She lays into me with the slapping and I try to laugh it off as her hands bat at me like table-tennis paddles. But then the hands turn to fists and some of the punches connect, and I realise that I've gone too far.

'*You* stupid!' she yells at me, pounding blows on my head and uppercuts to my jaw.

'Lily, stop it!'

'*You* stupid! You not see a good thing when you have it already!'

I'm still in my seat. I could stand up and walk away. She's a short, chubby middle-aged woman. I could outrun her. I could punch her, lay her out with one return blow. And who would blame me? But I don't. I writhe around and twist my arms like I've got ants in my clothes while Lily rains down blows from above.

'Lily, please, stop!' I cry out.

'FUCKIN' SHUT UP, I'M TRYING TO SLEEP IN 'ERE!' a grumpy male voice roars out from one of the huts.

Lily sits back down and composes herself. She pours herself coffee and her hand isn't even trembling, while I am a huddled, smashed-up wreck.

'I'm sorry,' I whisper. 'I'm sorry.'

She sips her coffee, lights a cigarette and gazes impassively towards the sea.

'I'm sorry,' I whisper again.

Lily reaches out for the plate of croissants and pulls it across the table away from me. 'No more croissant for you.' Then she slides the jug out of my reach. 'And definitely no orange juice.'

I swallow hard, fighting back tears.

Twenty-six

By the time I arrive at the hospital my face doesn't look as bad as Visser's does but I can feel a bruise on my cheek and a swollen lip. If Visser asks, I'm just going to tell him that I got drunk and punched myself in the face. Something he might understand. But he doesn't ask. He's far too interested in himself to notice anything much about me – which is good, because I'd rather not talk about it at all.

'So, what are they saying about me in cyberspace?' is the first thing he asks me when I sit down by the bed and take out my notebook.

'Don't you know? No smartphone?'

He rolls his eyes from one incapacitated arm to the other as if to say 'Duh!' 'In any case, it smashed when I fell.'

'But you were naked under your robe when they found you. Where was the phone?'

'My phone is always the first thing I reach for when I wake up. I must have taken it with me to the balcony.'

'In any case, you've had visitors. You're colleagues from the conference.' I make a point of stating this as a fact that I know for certain.

'Yes, I know what they are prepared to tell or not tell me and I understand their professional constraints,' he says impatiently. 'But I want your unique perspective as a journalist.'

I mentally list what I've learned so far from the likes of Laura, Mr Lau and Nick Davenport, and hope that it will create the desired impression that I've researched all this online.

'Some people say that you staged your accident deliberately as a publicity stunt for Extinction Rebellion.'

'Ha! What nonsense! How could one "stage" something like this? You should take a photo. Let them look at me. Ridiculous!'

Not having a camera, and not wishing to reveal that I have no smartphone, I ignore the invitation.

'Are you a member of Extinction Rebellion?'

Again, he laughs, though it costs him pain. 'Extinction Rebellion is not a club that you can choose to join or not join. You're already in it. We all are. We are the ones facing extinction. All of us. If we want to survive we must rebel. Our humanity compels us to it.'

'So you've participated in their protests?'

'Of course. I've spoken at their rallies. And if my accident brings publicity to their cause, then all well and good. Make sure you quote that in your article. But it had nothing to do with Extinction Rebellion, certainly not on my part.'

'Others are saying that it was a suicide attempt.'

Visser goes quiet for a few monitor beeps, and I begin to wonder if the drugs are zoning him out again. Then he says, 'Who?'

'I'm sorry?'

'Who is saying this?'

'Facebook,' I say for want of anyone more specific.

'Facebook!' his voice rumbles with disdain. 'Facebook is like staring at your own backside in a mirror, bent over and looking between your legs with your own cock and balls dangling in your face.'

Unless you're a female, I think, but don't say it.

'Do you want me to quote you on that too?'

'With pleasure. You know that half the people on your so-called "Friends" list are probably bots?' I try not to look stupid. 'Algorithms. They are not real people. Their only function is to make you buy or do something.'

I try to steer us away from technical stuff that I have no knowledge of by throwing him a real name.

'I spoke to a Dr Nicholas Davenport. He implied that your career is declining; that your ideas have fallen out of favour with the academic community.'

'Nick Davenport! The man is a dreamer. His ideas are naïve at best. At worst, he is a salesman, selling his toys to the biggest buyer.'

'Do you mean he's lying about you?'

'I'm saying he's wrong. My ideas are not in decline. They're on the rise. Their time is yet to come. But it will be soon. It must be soon.'

His rhetoric is that of a Bond villain, or Hitler. I don't know what his plans are for world salvation but I'm not ready to take him on in those terms yet.

'Is that what you were saying at the party? Was Davenport there that night?'

'Oh. The party. It was only a small party, a dozen delegates socialising and getting tight together. They should ban shop talk when alcohol is involved. My God, I could use a drink now!'

I remember the vodka in my satchel. 'Actually…'

He cottons on immediately. 'You haven't, have you?'

'But the drugs. Will they react?'

'What is it?'

I realise we are both whispering. I show him the vodka.

'Put a little in my water cup. Just enough to taste it.'

I look at him sceptically.

'It'll be fine,' he says. 'Trust me, I'm a doctor. I'm two doctors.'

I remove the lid and pour in a little glug and top it up with water. Then I help him drink.

'Thank you, Bob. You can help me finish that before you go.'

I put the cup back on the trolley for now, and watch Visser's demeanour relax like someone who's just successfully scratched a very bad itch.

'Tell me, Bob. Have you ever heard of a man called Norman Borlaug?'

'No. Who is he? A Nazi?'

'No. Quite the opposite. Norman Borlaug saved far more people than the Nazis ever killed. Over a billion, in fact. Yet no one has heard of him.'

I automatically think of Otto Schindler.

'What did he do?'

'Norman Borlaug – write it down, B, O, R, L, A, U, G – was a botanist and a geneticist. His doctorate from the University of Minnesota, I believe, was on botanical genetics and pathology. In the nineteen-forties and fifties he developed new crop strains that saved people from starvation in Mexico, India and Pakistan, three of the most heavily populated countries on earth. In doing so, he also enabled the global population to triple to what it is now, nearly seven billion, in just half a century. Which is why, at this "party" you are talking about, I expressed the view that the history books – the only place in which his name is remembered – should be rewritten to brand him as the criminal he was.'

'I don't understand. How is that a crime?'

'Think about it, Bob. What is the biggest problem facing the planet right now?'

'Plastic?'

'Not even close.'

'Logging? Fracking? Air travel?'

'Bob, Bob, Bob – it's none of those things. It's all of those things. It's us. It's… children. Overpopulation is the driving factor behind all the world's problems today. And it doesn't matter how many trees we replant or what methods we find to harness clean energy or neutralise greenhouse gases. We *can* feed the world, but only at the cost of our own extinction. We are eating and fucking ourselves to death. And if there is an architect behind the extermination of the entire human race, his name is Norman Borlaug.'

'Have you said that to his face?'

'He died ten years ago. But as a matter of fact, yes, I did. Well, in a letter.'

'What did he say?'

'He never replied. And now they call him the father of the Green Revolution. Fools. I'm sorry, Bob. I don't mean to sound bitter.'

'So you said all that at the party, to this gathering of pissed intellectuals in the all-night bar?'

'Like I said. Shop talk and alcohol don't mix. Give me some more of that water, will you?' I help him to more of the drink. 'But of course, that is why we were all there. To exchange ideas, debate our opinions; to brainstorm. Otherwise, why did we all expel many tons of CO_2 into the atmosphere to get there?'

'And Davenport didn't like it?'

'Davenport is a corporate lackey. I didn't say that to his face but he knows what I think of him. But, yes, let's say he was my most vociferous critic that night.'

'Did you fight?'

'No, Bob. There was no *brawling*.' He relishes the word, showing off his knowledge of the English idiom. 'We are scientists, intellectuals; not little boys in the schoolyard.'

I decide to play my card.

'Dr Visser. Do you know a woman called Laura Duxton? Could she have been with you that night?'

'Is she a delegate?'

'I think so. I think she may have replaced another speaker at the last minute.'

Visser thinks for a moment. 'I can't think of anyone by that name. But that means nothing. She may have been there. There were a number of faces I couldn't put a name to. Do you have a photo of her?'

'I'm afraid I don't. She'll have known Davenport. They used to work together, maybe still do.'

'Davenport was with a woman. A young girl, really.'

'Kristina,' I say. 'Blonde. His… assistant.'

Visser seems to comprehend the subtext of my pregnant pause.

'Yes. She was with him. But there was no other woman with him. What does this Laura Duxton look like?'

'Slim. Pale complexion. Long dark hair, shoulder-length, possibly pushed back with a band. Mid-thirties.'

'I'm sorry, Bob, there wasn't anyone there like that.'

'No worries,' I say. In fact, I'm glad. It's one less deception to accuse her of, if or when the time comes.

'Why is she important?'

'It's just another angle I'm working on.'

'I thought your story was about me.'

I like Visser but he likes himself even more, which would seem to rule him out as the suicidal type. He might be on some unfashionable, politically incorrect, crypto-eugenic crusade but I don't see him as a willing martyr to it.

'It is about you, Dr Visser,' I assure him.

This is probably a lie. There is a story here but I'm not sure it's the one I want to tell. 'When are you getting out of here?'

'I don't know. No time soon, I think. Tell me, Bob, do you have a family?'

I flash on my mum and dad and feel my skin go cold.

'You mean here?'

'Yes. A wife. Children.'

'No.'

Visser looks thoughtful, taking his time to absorb my very short, specific answer. His eyes shift to the window.

'Good. Good man.'

I almost ask him the same but the veil of regret over his expression tells me not to go there. After a while, he looks at the water cup then at me, and I help him finish his drink.

'Dr Visser, I'm sorry but I have to ask you again. You said yourself that you'd been drinking till the early hours the night before, and that you woke up early to close the curtains when the accident occurred. Do you wish me to conclude that alcohol was not a factor?'

He looks me in the eye. 'Yes. I do. Write this down: I was not drunk and I am not stupid.'

I do as he says, just for effect.

As I'm about to leave, I pull my Columbo routine and ask him one final question that might move things on instead of stopping at a dead end. My next gambit.

'If I speak to Dr Davenport again, is there anything you'd like me to say to him on your behalf?'

Visser grins and calls me back in.

Twenty-seven

I double back to the conference venue on the bike, hoping to be able to catch Nick Davenport doing the rounds. It's the closing day of the conference and the foyer remains open to the public. I stand around enjoying the air-con, pretending to look at the exhibits and keeping one eye on my watch and the other on the doorway to the conference chambers. At noon, the inner vestibule fills up with delegates as they emerge for a breather from their talks.

I don't really care whether Laura spots me or not, but once again I fail to see her anywhere among them. After a while, Davenport spots me, though, and makes his excuses to the bald East Asian man he's talking with to come over to me, with Kristina his dainty minder in tow.

'Mister—' he begins.

'Lorrimer,' says Kristina.

Are they splitting sentences now, in some bizarre double act?

'Bob,' I say.

'You're back.' Davenport gets through this one solo. 'What happened to you?'

I remember my face, the bruise and the split lip.

'Oh, it was dumb. I fell over at home this morning putting my trousers on. I knew I should've sat down.'

'The most common cause of accidents in the home.'

'Is it really?'

'Did you visit Professor Visser?'

'I did. And it's just "Doctor", apparently. He doesn't like "Professor". Says it makes him sound like – Felix the Cat?' I smile good-humouredly, inviting false bonhomie.

'Indeed. Pieter has his foibles.'

He grins at Kristina and she dutifully grins at me until we are all grinning at one another. That Pieter, eh?

'And how is he?'

'You haven't visited him?'

'No. Is he all right?'

'He'll live. He may even be up and walking soon. He was lucky not to break his legs or pelvis, I guess.' I change my tone to act a little shocked and disapproving: 'He told me some of the stuff he was coming out with in the bar the night before the accident. About some guy Borlaug being a war criminal or something?'

'Not a war criminal but an "architect of total human genocide", I believe was the clincher. It's ludicrous, of course. Borlaug was a humanitarian, perhaps the greatest the world has ever known. He received the Nobel Peace prize, for God's sake. And Pieter Visser wanted us all to go to Iowa and rewrite his headstone.'

'I agree, it's pretty strong stuff. So how heated did this argument get?'

'I wouldn't go so far as to call it an argument. We were debating vigorously.'

'But there was some heavy drinking.'

Davenport narrows his eyes at me.

'I won't deny, we were in our cups. It's not illegal.'

'No, of course not. Visser thinks he stirred up some resentment, though.' I improvise a bit of journalese. 'Would you care to comment on that?'

'I might,' he says, 'if you'd care to show me that press pass of yours again.'

My heart starts jumping and I hope I don't turn red. Luckily, my skin is naturally quite dark, a pale olive, and further tanned by the local climate, hopefully concealing any blush response.

I take the pass from my pocket and hand it to him and he scrutinises it for what feels like a full minute. Then he hands it back and smiles. Kristina looks relieved over his shoulder.

'If it's a quote you're looking for, how about this? Pieter Visser is a respected environmentalist whose academic views I don't always agree with. He disagrees, for instance, that technology will one day be capable of filtering CO_2 from the air, while I believe it will soon become a reality. But what happened to him was awful. Neither I nor anyone I know would wish or intend him any harm, and we pray for his full and speedy recovery.'

Davenport is ready to end the interview there but I stop him in mid-turn.

'Dr Visser told me to ask you about your work for the British government.'

He pauses like a gecko near a fly.

'My work as an adviser to the government is already well-documented. But what of it?'

'Visser said that your reports to the Environmental Audit Committee were – "redacted" was the word he used.'

This stirs Davenport and his eyes harden. 'Pieter Visser lives and works in the Netherlands. What's the British government's business got to do with him?'

'Nick…' Kristina steps forward and puts her hand on his arm. I've clearly shaken him, but he lets her hand rest where it is, a calming touchstone.

'Britain's still in the EU, isn't it?' I say. Secretly, I'm not quite sure if it is or not, hoping he takes the question tag as rhetorical.

'Not for much longer.'

'But is there any truth in it? He claims that top climate scientists are scared to tell governments how bad it really is for fear of losing funding and consultancies. It's public knowledge that it's happened before. Respected scientists discredited because their findings don't support the government's agenda.'

'I refuse to comment on that.'

He turns away dismissively and Kristina takes his arm, but then he twists away from her and back to me with anger in his eyes.

'Except to say that if you print any of that I shall sue Pieter Visser and I shall sue the *Straits Times*.'

He strides away with Kristina trotting to keep up.

'Dr Davenport!' I call out my final question, the only one that really matters: 'Do you know a woman named Laura Duxton?'

He doesn't stop, doesn't turn around, doesn't falter in his retreat, just flicks an impatient hand at me over his shoulder.

'Never heard of her.'

I cannot see whether Davenport shows any facial reaction. But I glimpse Kristina's concerned profile looking up at him as she catches up to march in step with him; and, at the mention of Laura's name, nothing in it alters, or betrays any sign of recognition.

Twenty-eight

On my way to lunch back in town I go into a tourist shop that sells foreign newspapers to see which English ones they stock. I peruse the titles on the racks, all of them yesterday's editions, and immediately dismiss the slew of red-tops. I have a quick shufti through the pages of the *Daily Express* and put it back. Then I gather up *The Times*, *The Guardian* and *The Telegraph* and take them to the counter to pay for them.

I make an unholy mess of the table top with them in the backstreet canteen where I go to eat, and the locals complain when all the rustling interferes with their telenovela. So when I'm done eating I take myself off to Danny's and sit with a coffee by the beach, where the breeze makes a mess of them instead. When I finally get it all under control, I have three articles that I've found, one in each paper.

The *Times* and *Telegraph* articles are little more than a paragraph each, one headed 'ASEAN Climate Conference Opens' and the other, 'ASEAN to Debate Climate This Weekend'. They seem to have been taken verbatim from the same news wire and neither one tells me anything I don't already know: the basic when, where and what for, and, without naming any of them, that several British climate experts are among the key speakers.

The article from *The Guardian* has a little more meat to it. The headline reads 'Climate Conference Opens Following Accident'. As well as giving the same information as the other two, it reports the sketchy details of the balcony incident and alludes to the online Extinction Rebellion rumour but leaves out any speculations about suicide.

It then goes on to namecheck, interestingly, Dr Nicholas Davenport of Cambridge University's Department of Earth Sciences, with a seat on the government's Environmental

Audit Committee, who, seven years ago, was embroiled in a legal dispute over a patent with 'Prof' Visser.

In the newspaper story, Davenport's presence at the same conference is brought on as an interesting side coincidence. But in my mind it confirms that these two are old rivals, like Edison and Tesla, still fighting the same duel over intellectual property rights, and I can't think of a good reason why I would want to get myself any more involved in their personal feud.

The story now is all Laura. With Davenport, it was hard to tell, but Kristina showed no reaction to Laura's name. I can understand his denying he knows her. He was hardly in the mood to resume a conversation with me about anything, and he certainly wouldn't want to lose face by having to discuss his ex-partner in front of his current lover. But for Kristina to indicate no knowledge of Laura's name and no curiosity as to why I brought it up is inexplicable if, as Laura claims, they all work together in the same department.

I sit back for a moment and have a little chuckle about it all, imagining what Dr Davenport would think if he knew he had let himself be rattled by a local taxi cyclist of no consequence. If I happen to see him in town tonight, maybe I'll stop and tout for his custom just to see the look on his face.

The upshot is that I was right all along. Laura is not who she pretends to be. She isn't attached to the conference, and very likely has nothing to do with Pieter Visser's accident either. I can't see any reason why she would. And, unless my intuition is wrong or he and Kristina know her by a different name, she has no connection to Nick Davenport. Which only leaves me with theory number three.

This *is* about me.

Twenty-nine

It's not that Cory Stewart was a bully. Bullies are social losers, and cowards at heart. They bully because it's what they know at home, and they're scared of any finer feelings. But Cory's dad never laid a hand on him, nor his mum. If they had, Cory would have told me, or I would have sensed it. We were close like that. The fact that he let me be close was part of his charisma.

But Cory had a cruel streak running through him; plus, he was clever with it. He was an adult before his time, knew how to manipulate grown-ups without wheedling at them like a child. He spoke in tones that made them listen. Honeyed tones.

His number one response, when accused of something awful that he'd done, was a measured and reassuring 'Sorry, Mum, I don't know anything about it'. The template adroitly fitted all sizes. 'Sorry, Mum/Dad/Miss/Sir/Officer, I don't know anything about it.' And it epitomised Cory's talent for self-serving deception.

I often wondered how he always managed to pull the wool over his parents' eyes and get away with it. It was only later that I learned how much they were prepared to collude in the illusion that he had.

We lived in a small village that had been gratefully overlooked for redevelopment as a dormer town for nearby cities like Sheffield and Doncaster. Most of the houses were stone-built and ancient. We lived in one of the red-brick houses on what locals still called the 'new' estate, which had been new fifteen years before I was born. My dad was a 'Yorkshireman, born and bred' who worked in a steel foundry until it closed down, then he got on with his gardening, fishing and sitting in the village pub a lot. My mum was of Mediterranean stock: her grandparents migrated from Greece some time just before or after the Second World

War. She was a hairdresser, the village hairdresser in fact, making house calls to regular clients and enjoying cups of tea and the local gossip.

I guess I regarded them as 'simple folk', a phrase I learned from a bedtime story when I was a nipper. Home life was unruffled, my parents loved me and each other, and family stability gave me the kind of comfort an only child like me required. Cory and his sister Katy and their mum and dad lived just a few doors down, I was always in and out of their house, and they looked like a normal family too.

All the other schoolkids thought Cory was cool, and I did too when he wasn't being a jerk. I had known him since we moved there when I was seven, so all through primary school and into the first years of secondary. I was a year younger than him, which may account for the scorn he sometimes treated me with, but because we lived on the same street – and because our two sets of parents got on so well – I was literally his closest friend.

Most of the time he wasn't nasty at all. He was funny, and daring, and knowledgeable about all kinds of stuff. Where to see dome-shaped nests of long-tailed tits, or pipistrelle bats roosting in the day. Where to catch fish without a net or line. Where to find the best conkers before the autumn term began. How to grasp a nettle without being stung. He knew the names of lots of plants, insects, birds and wildflowers and could tell you their yearly life cycle and even make a joke out of them that would make you laugh.

One summer we started building a treehouse together in the woods and got quite far on with it. We worked well together and though Cory designed it, and told me where to put what, he wasn't bossy about it. He wanted to finish it and knew that being bossy would risk him losing my help. But at some point, I got bored. I began to see the impossibility of finishing it before the end of the holiday. Cory got cross; he got coercive. Said I was supposed to be his best friend, wasn't I, and insisted that we bust our guts to complete it in time. I said we could carry on at weekends and still get it finished before Bonfire Night. It wasn't that I didn't want to finish it, just that I wanted a break. Secretly, also, I refused to let him force me like a slave. He told me dismissively that he would finish it by himself, and I think he did try.

Then, one dry afternoon, the unfinished treehouse burnt down, no culprits apprehended. The fire brigade had to come, and a policeman came to our house and asked me and my parents a lot of questions before finally going away. I felt sick that we'd done all that work for nothing. Just because I wanted to do something else with my time and Cory didn't like it. Of course, when the police called on the Stewarts it was, 'Sorry, Constable, I don't know anything about it,' with staunch parental backing.

Cory avoided me for the remainder of the holidays, letting me lick my wounds and kick my heels alone and disconsolate, but then acted like nothing had happened when school resumed. It was always like that if I did something to upset him. He'd find some way to punish me that a bully wouldn't be clever enough to think of. But the moment I sensed the light of his forgiveness, I would immediately slip gratefully back into his shadow.

Looking back, it's clear to me that Cory must have been one of those people who feel no empathy for others because a part of their brain never properly developed. I read about that once in a magazine or newspaper but I've forgotten the technical terms. It only affects one or two percent of us, but they're the ones who are most likely to become violent psychopaths and serial killers. Not all of them are highly intelligent; habitual thugs can't be because their attitude does nothing in others but breed resentment against them. But Cory was. I think he used his intelligence as the bedrock of his charm and credibility, because no one resented Cory, not even me.

Sometimes, there was no accounting for the things he did. He did some things purely to see what would happen, or for a private laugh at a result only he would see a funny side to. Like the time we were climbing out of the back of his dad's car after his dad picked us up from some fine outing we'd just enjoyed together, and Cory shut the door on my leg. Naturally, he said it was an accident and his dad believed him, but I knew it was done on purpose. Like he'd just wanted to test his own strength to see if he could break the bone. He didn't. Maybe something inside him made him hold back a last ounce of strength, though I doubt it. Whatever that something is, inside Cory there was only an empty space there. Growing up, I'd seen how cruel he could be to certain creatures he didn't like, such as wasps and spiders. He once caught a mouse in a bucket and scalded it to death with boiling water from the kettle. Why? To see what would happen.

At other times, his acts were motivated by petulance, like the burning of the treehouse, or by a desire to get even for something. One time, walking home after a school fayre, where I had succeeded in winning a goldfish and he had not, he slapped the polythene bag out of my hand and the fish died. I started crying over the limp dead fish on the palm of my hand, couldn't help it. I expected Cory to make fun of my tears but he didn't. Instead, he said he was sorry, that he didn't mean to kill it. How could he *not* have killed it? But I knew they were only words, spoken to keep me in his thrall. This was an integral aspect of the pattern of his errant behaviour. He would see how far he could push me around and still be able to get back in my good books.

Even my own parents colluded in his efforts, convincing me that he didn't mean to do whatever it was he'd done, and persuading me to forgive him. I didn't understand why they weren't sticking up for me, why they always took his side or gave him the benefit of the doubt. They made out like they were doing me a favour, preserving a friendship whose preciousness I would not truly appreciate until it was gone. It was as if they were desperate for Cory and me to stay friends.

The crazy thing is, I wanted us to. Cory was the only other kid in the village who took any interest in me.

Sometimes, it was the kind of interest that a teacher shows in a willing student. He taught me how to build a den in the bushes, how to hang upside down from a rope-swing, how to suck nectar from clover flowers. At other times, it was more like the interest a vivisectionist shows in a lab rat.

I was always cautious, for instance, if things started getting rough and tumble because what began as fun invariably ended with dead-legs, camel bites, Chinese burns and other tortures that he would inflict, not just to prove his dominance but also to witness my reaction. When the laughter stopped, his face took on the blank aspect of cold-hearted curiosity as he punched my arm again. Any resulting bruises were laughed off at home by my simple folks as being all in a day's boys' adventure out in the woods and fields. As I got older, I stopped my parents from seeing the bruises. I would rather hide them than listen to their dismissals. It's not like it happened that often anyway. And once I got a bit bigger, any day now, I would surprise him by fighting back...

Thirty

These thoughts fizzle out when I see Laura walking down the beach towards me. I tidy up the newspapers and fold them away under my chair.

'What's up? Did the conference finish early?'

'No, but I did. I think I've got all I wanted out of it.'

She sits down at my table and I wonder when to tell her that I know she's a liar.

But do I know this yet completely? Davenport said he didn't know her name and Kristina showed no response. But, supposing for a moment that she really is Davenport's ex – does Kristina know that? Or has Davenport – and, by implication, Laura – kept their prior relationship a secret from her? That could explain Kristina's blank response, which is really all I've got to go on.

I'm back where I was before. If I don't have the facts straight, if Laura can reasonably dispute my suspicions about her, I will have tipped my hand and lost all chance of ever reaching the truth.

'Fuck, Mike! What happened to you?'

I remember the state of my face from Lily's fists.

'I fell off the bike.' My third untrue explanation if you include the one I prepared for Visser. 'Nothing serious.'

She looks at my arms and legs. 'You were lucky. No grazes.'

'Just a light face-dive. I'll live.'

Once that's been established, she pins me with a serious look.

'Mike, there's something I need to ask you. Yesterday, when you introduced me to Danny, the guy at the beach bar, you told him I was Laura Duxton. But I never told you my surname. How did you know it?'

I decide that the truth, or a version of it, is the best option.

'From Lily. She saw it on your passport.'

130

'Did you ask her or did she mention it?'

I sense the future riding on my answer.

'I asked.'

'Why?'

'Because I'm interested in you. Because I like you. And I wanted to know if you had a cool surname or a naff surname.'

She laughs. 'And which is it?'

'On the coolometer, I'd give it a six,' I say, hoping she doesn't ask me mine, in which case, 'Hammer' is right out and I'll have to say something else quick.

'I think it's a bit naff,' she says. 'I dropped it for a long time after— Oh, it's a long story, and not a very happy one.'

I reach across the table and take her hand.

'What?'

'When I was seventeen I fell in love with a boy. I didn't mention him before when you asked if there was anyone special before Nick because it's all rather sad and a bit embarrassing. He was a soldier, like my father – who didn't approve at all, by the way. But I was a defiant little sod and we were crazy about each other and wanted to marry and raise kids together, so we got married and I became Mrs Duxton. We had five good months until Tony fucking Blair deployed his regiment to Iraq. He never returned. Well – his body. After the funeral I reverted to my maiden name, but years later, after Nick and I split up, I decided to go back to my married name.'

'I'm sorry,' I say, rubbing her hand. The question is dangling there: what maiden name? But I dare not ask it.'Something like that,' I say mindlessly, 'at such a young age...'

'It lives with you forever. A love frozen in time. But let's not descend into clichés, I'm sure if he'd come back alive, we would not have lived happily ever after. I would have had a very different life, and not one that I would envy now. But I was a teenager. I bounced back and was determined to make good of myself.'

I can't decide whether her story brings clarity or adds further obfuscation to her past.

'When are you leaving?' I say.

I realise I'm still holding her hand. Her fingers squeeze mine.

'Not yet.'

'Good.'

Thirty-one

We dine out together again that night. Afterwards, Laura says, 'Let's go dancing. It's the first morning tomorrow that I don't have to get up.'

'I'm not much of a dancer. I don't go in for house music. But I'll take you to a place that I do like, if you're up for it.'

I take her to a club much farther down the beach and her arms wrap around my waist on the back of the bike. I'm not drinking tonight, I want to keep a clear head, and not just for the road. The club is called Igloo. It's housed in an ugly whitewashed dome that from a distance reminds me of the military listening post at Fylingdale. 'The Golf Balls', we used to call them; when I was a kid.

Inside, through the short tunnel entrance, it's all smoke and lasers and the DJ is playing something slow, rhythmic and wistful. The domed ceiling space is festooned with baffles like a sailing ship, but with a mirror ball for a crow's nest. Shadows of dancers weave and sway in the fog to the ambient music. The periphery of the circular space is lined with twinkling settees, not all of them occupied.

'The DJs only play chill-out music here,' I say without the need to shout.

'Cool.'

We grab a settee and I bring us some drinks from the bar, a beer for her and a blackcurrant and soda water for me. The prices aren't outrageous, which is another reason I knew I liked this place, though I need to be careful now with what cash I've got left.

'Can you get hold of any drugs?' she asks me, to my surprise. I don't see her as a druggie at all, though of course, it's hard to say what I see her as.

'I don't do drugs,' I tell her.

'That's not what I asked. I asked if you can get any.'

I think of Panda and his fondness for spliff. Then I think of how much he would not appreciate my bringing a new stranger into his world.

'I don't know anywhere,' I say carefully. 'I don't mix with those kinds of people.'

She seems to ponder this for a moment.

'Tell me honestly, Mike. What are you doing here? You're – what? Approaching forty? You have no girlfriend, no family, no attachments here. You earn barely enough to scrape by, and God knows how you do that out of the tourist season. What's keeping you here?'

'I—'

'Or what are you hiding from?'

We're tiptoeing at the edge of a minefield, and it's Laura who's guiding us into it. I had the feeling that it should be me leading but that feeling has morphed into a big scary chasm.

'I... did something when I was younger that I'm not particularly proud of. Let's just leave it at that.'

She looks puzzled. 'Haven't we all?'

'Not like this. Please, leave it.'

'Well, what was it? It can't be that bad? You're not on the run from the law, are you?'

'No, of course not. Please, Laura, I'm not ready to talk about it.'

'But you've got me worried now.'

'No, no, it was nothing—'

I want to tell her she's safe with me, that it wasn't a sex crime or anything like that, but know that it would just sound creepy and not reassuring at all.

'It happened when I was a child. Look, I'm not going into details because I don't like to think about it. There was an incident, another kid got hurt and I feel guilty about it. Okay? End of story.'

She stays silent for a few beats.

'And is that why you're here, then, hidden away and living like a pauper? Because you feel guilty about something that happened when you were a child?'

I think she takes it for a Buddhist thing; that I'm working out some already long-paid penance or karma.

'I'm here because there are people I can't face. And one of them is me.'

I don't mean it to sound self-pitying, and I hope she isn't pitying me when she leans into my shoulder and kisses me on the mouth.

'Let's dance,' she says.

We smooch in each other's arms on the edge of the dance floor to something mystical and lush, and light-beams spangle on our faces. We don't talk. We don't do much but shuffle in small circles and gaze into each other's eyes until Laura softly pushes my head down onto her shoulder, then we shuffle some more like that until the music changes, which it never does.

'Let's go home,' I say.

She doesn't say it's early. She doesn't say she wants another drink. She doesn't say anything but 'Okay'.

We leave our drinks and go back to Laura's hut. She's made it a homely nest with a few scattered things from her suitcase but neither of us is interested in talking interior décor. We start kissing standing up, our hands all over each other, and tumble together onto the bed with our lips locked. But when I reach behind her to unzip her dress I realise that something's off.

'Mike…'

She turns her face away and her body goes rigid.

'Mike, I'm sorry, I can't do this. It isn't right.'

I stop what I'm doing and lean up on my elbow to look at her.

'What's wrong?'

'I'm sorry, Mike, it doesn't feel right. Mike, I haven't been totally honest with you.'

This is it, I think. Here it comes.

'I still have feelings for Nick.' Some look that she sees on my face puts her on the defensive. 'I know I should let myself get over him, but I can't.'

I feel like I've just had one of those orgasms that builds and builds but melts away before the climax. I separate myself from her on the bed and stand up.

'I see.'

'I'm sorry.'

'No. Really. Don't be.' I pick up my satchel. 'I'm gonna go now.'

'You don't have to. We can sit and talk. Or we can go back out.'

'No, Laura, no, I really can't.'

I leave it at that. There's nothing more to say. I walk out.

I don't go straight back to my hut in case Laura might hear me from across the divide. These huts are anything but sound-proof. Instead, I walk down to the beach where it's distant and quiet, and take out the Motorola. There's one last, honest question I need to put to Nick Davenport before he leaves the island. I get a woman on reception.

'Shiri Palace.'

'I need to speak with a guest there, Dr Nicholas Davenport. Can you put me through to his room, please?'

'Which room number?'

'I'm sorry, I don't know the room number.'

There's a moment of silence while she looks at her screen.

'Ah, yes. Two-two-eight. Putting you through.'

I nearly drop the phone when the significance of that number hits me. I think about hanging up but I really want to ask him my question. I listen to the burr of the 'ringing' tone until the receptionist comes back on the line.

'Sorry, no reply.'

I hang up, my mind veering back to a different track, Laura momentarily forgotten.

So Nick Davenport was in room 228 all along. Right next door to Pieter Visser, in 227. I recall their feud from the newspaper article, an accusation that Davenport had stolen Visser's work, which was ultimately not upheld by the courts. And I recall Visser's broken phone found next to him on the slabs below his balcony. Bandura and the local constabulary might have been too lax or too lazy to put two and two together, or they may not have even seen the numbers; but I have.

I just need to check one more thing. I phone Shiri Palace again and get the same receptionist.

'Could you check on another conference guest for me? Perhaps she can connect me to Dr Davenport. Could you give me her room number?'

'What name, please?'

'It's Kristina. I don't know the second name.'

'One moment, I'll look.'

I wait, hoping that there's only one Kristina on the guest register.

'Ah, here she is. Kristina Blixen, room three-oh-one. Would you like me to put you through?'

The receptionist has just given me the information I wanted. But if there's a chance that Davenport is there in Kristina's room right now and I can put my question about Laura to him, or even to Kristina...

'Yes, please.'

It rings but there is no reply and after a while I hang up.

It occurred to me that if Davenport and Kristina were both here on an academic or corporate junket they would take full advantage by separately booking a room each, and now I've confirmed that Kristina's room is on a different floor with a different overlook, well away from Davenport's room. Visser would surely have worked out in the bar that night that the two of them were sleeping together, and it wouldn't take much to check that they went back to her room and not his.

So that's what Visser was doing...!

I feel like I've solved one mystery, and that it might make a good subplot for a book. If I get the chance, I'll go back to the hospital and confront Visser with it. I don't know what good it will do other than to give me a little peace of mind by tidying up a loose end.

But as I put this to bed, my question for Nick Davenport burns at the front of my brain again. I can't let him leave without my knowing. I lift the phone and redial the number by moonlight to give it one last shot. I prepare to put on a different voice if necessary but luckily I get a different receptionist, a guy this time.

'Hello,' I say, 'this is the taxi service for Mr Davenport in room two-two-eight. I'm phoning to confirm that his booking to the airport is for tomorrow.'

I wait while the receptionist checks.

'That's correct.'

'Can you tell me which flight he is on?'

'Sorry, we don't have that information.'

'What time is he checking out?'

'Normal checkout is eleven. Which taxi service is calling, please?'

I hang up.

I can do one of two things. I can accept that I've missed my chance, and let it go. Or I can find out which flight Davenport is taking and hope to catch him at the airport before he gets on it.

I walk back up through the huts all the way to the front and get on the bike and ride along the strip to May's snack bar. It's not so late, and the place is still open, and lively with regular customers. Kenny is there, smoking at one of the tables and playing an old guy at chess.

'Have you seen Amnat?' I ask him.

'I think he's in the back.'

I go through. Amnat is sitting drinking with some buddies. I beckon him aside.

'If I was going back to England tomorrow,' I ask him, 'which flight would I take from here to make the smoothest connection?'

'You leaving us, Mike?'

'No. It's not for me, it's for someone else. One of the British conference delegates. Which flight would they be on?'

He smiles uncomfortably at his knowledge being tested this way, but I place my bet on his familiarity with the schedules.

'I don't know, Mike. So many airlines connect to UK... You know which airport?'

I once spent two whole days poring over a map of Great Britain in a library book, trying to work out where I was being held. I close my eyes to cast my mind back to that map, trying to think of a large enough airport close to Cambridge.

'Stansted! Are there flights that connect to Stansted?'

Amnat thinks hard and comes up with a couple of likely flight times from the island, one mid-morning and one in the late afternoon.

'Thanks, Amnat, you're a star.'

'Your friend wanna book me to airport?'

I don't want to slap him in the face after he's just helped me out so I lie to him instead. 'I'll ask.'

Thirty-two

I rise early the next morning and skip breakfast with Lily. I want to get away before Laura shows herself. It's obvious that Lily knows something is amiss, what with her sixth sense and that bat hearing of hers, but she doesn't say anything to me that she hasn't already said, and knows that it's too late to say anything else.

I take the bike and ride it out to the airport. I skirt past where taxis and riders are waiting in the already blazing heat for new arrivals and park up in the departures zone. Here, buses and coaches pull up and disgorge streams of homebound holidaymakers. I spend an hour pacing up and down, scouring the sunburnt faces under all the hats for a sign of Nick Davenport or Kristina Blixen. Finally, a large touring coach packed with the first of the departing conference delegates swings into view, and there the two of them are, filing off with their hand luggage.

I run over to them.

'Dr Davenport!'

He turns around. His expression shrivels from expectation to disdain when he sees who's calling his name.

'Not you again! Bloody sod off, Lorrimer – ' He casts a withering eye over my new appearance, unshaven in shorts and a T-shirt. 'Or whoever you are.'

'It's not about you, or Pieter Visser. That isn't the story. Please, Dr Davenport. I need your help. Just one question, please.'

I shuffle along next to him in the moving queue like a persistent beggar. In a moment, airport security will prevent me from following him any farther.

'What is it, then?' he says tetchily.

I glance at Kristina.

'I asked you if you knew a woman called Laura Duxton. You may have known her as Laura Stewart.'

He sighs. 'It rings no bells.'

'Or Katy Stewart.'

'You're pushing it now. But no, I don't know her.'

I can see that Kristina has no idea who I'm talking about.

'I'm talking about an old girlfriend? Or perhaps a student of yours?'

'Look, for the last time, I don't know her.'

I can see that I'm pissing him off again and he has no way of escape except with measured progress towards the building. Before he vanishes through the door I feel I owe him some form of apology or recompense.

'I'm sorry if I've been a nuisance, Dr Davenport. I give you my word, I'm not going to write anything about you.'

He tosses back one last surly look at me as Kristina guides him by the elbow into the departure hall.

I return to my bike and head across the island to the hospital. On the journey I keep having to force myself to concentrate on the road instead of on the thoughts whirling in my head. The inland route from the airport to the capital passes dilapidated roadside villages, untouched by tourism, interspersed among banana plantations and paddy-fields grazing with water buffalo. It's a side of the island I seldom get to see but today I barely notice any of it. I'm too distracted thinking about Katy Stewart.

Katy was Cory Stewart's little sister. I was secretly sweet on her from about the age of ten, before I knew anything about crushes or puppy love, and managed to keep my feelings about her a secret from everyone. Towards the end of my friendship with Cory, Katy was the one compelling reason I kept up the charade that I wanted anything to do with him. I couldn't bear not being able to go round to their house and see her pretty face smile at me, or never have her accompany us on our adventures in the woods and fields.

She was there with us on the day in the woods when a naked man popped out of the bushes in front of us, and Cory, reacting quickly and sensibly, turned us around and ushered us away into the safety of the open meadow beyond the tree line where the man would not follow. I felt bonded with both of them after that experience.

She was nine years old when I did the thing that I did to Cory. Cory was thirteen and I was twelve and Katy was nine. And she was there when it happened. But she was too young to testify in court. At the time, I was too young to know how the system worked, only that I was caught in it, and I couldn't understand why she didn't tell them what she knew. She was there. She kind of witnessed it. I did it for her...

When I get to the hospital, Visser is sitting propped as upright in bed as he can be within the confines of the steel contraption supporting his potted arm. The monitor has been disconnected and stands silent. The bandage around his head has been replaced by a simple sticking-plaster, allowing his mop of hair to fall free. The bruising on his face has faded a little to purple and yellow and I can begin to see what he really looks like.

'You're looking better,' I say.

'You should have taken my photo yesterday.'

'I've left my camera at home. I brought this, though.'

I take out *The Guardian*, folded open at the relevant page, and read him the bit about him and Davenport going at it in court several years ago over an allegedly stolen idea.

'You knew that Davenport wasn't in his room that morning. And you said, yourself, that there was no one else around in the courtyard below.'

Visser looks uncomfortable. He tries to wriggle into a different position without causing himself extra pain.

'So?'

I pause, wondering what to lead with.

'It was the phone that gave it away, Doc. No one picks up their phone to walk across the bedroom to close the curtains. Didn't anyone else query that? The police?'

'A policeman interviewed me here the next day but I was too groggy to tell him much. He went away and hasn't come back since. But if he does, I will tell him exactly what I have told you.'

The old Cory Stewart denial. *Sorry, Officer, I don't know anything about it.*

'That's what you were doing, though, wasn't it? You were trying to climb across from your balcony to Davenport's. Maybe you noticed that his window was open, the curtain wafting through it. You could have seen that, leaning out. You went back in for your phone, maybe even knocked on Davenport's door to make sure his room was empty. Then you tried to cross, didn't you? What were you going to do? I doubt it was to take a selfie shitting on his bed. More likely search for documents and photograph stuff he was working on. Oh, it's okay, Dr Visser, relax. I'm not going to put any of this in print. You have my word.'

Visser's pomp has deflated but he looks oddly relieved.

'I'm not going to confirm or deny any of that. If that means no coverage in the *Straits Times*, then so be it.'

'Dr Visser, I'm not even a journalist. I never have been. I was only ever interested in the story of the woman I asked you about. Laura Duxton. Or maybe Laura Stewart. Or Katy Stewart. It doesn't matter, anyway. You don't know her, and that's the end of it.'

'So none of it was about me?'

'Just be happy that your secret is safe with me, Dr Visser. I know what Nick Davenport is like, and he's an arsehole.' I gather up my things to leave. 'But maybe cut Norman Borlaug some slack, eh? The poor guy was only trying to be helpful.'

At the door, I wish him well and we say goodbye on what I hope are equable terms.

Thirty-three

I don't know why I picked up that hammer out of Dad's toolbox that day. Dad was out in the garden mending a bit of trellis or something and I just saw it and lifted it as I walked by on my way out to play.

Cory and I were going across woods and fields to look for an old barn he'd heard about from some kid at school. You never knew what implements might be useful on such an expedition, and Dad's hammer was just the right size and weight for me to carry a long distance, and I didn't think he would mind me borrowing it if he noticed it was gone.

But that wasn't it, really. Something else told me to take it. Fate. Bad karma. And something else told me to stuff it down my waistband, out of plain sight from Cory, until the right moment when it would be needed.

When Cory said Katy was coming with us, I was secretly delighted but I could tell that Cory was pissed off about it. He'd wanted it to be just the two of us, a more controllable dynamic than three. But his parents insisted he take his little sister with him because they wanted the house to themselves for a few hours. That's what they said. I was there. I remember it distinctly. *We want the house to ourselves for a few hours.*

The disused barn was pretty far away. It took us a good half hour crossing wildflower meadows and striding over rippling streams to reach it. It was a hot sunny day and I'd drunk a lot of water before coming out of the house, thinking I was being sensible. Little did I know, however, that Katy was going to be with us, and by the time we reached the ramshackle old structure I was dying for a piss.

I looked around the inside of the barn, noting nettles sprouting in the corners, pigeons nesting and cooing in the rafters with shit everywhere, and a rusty old cattle trough standing off to one side. It must have been a cowshed. The trough looked like a urinal but there was no way I was pissing in that, not in front of Katy.

Cory noticed me dancing and crossing my legs.

'What's wrong with you?' he said.

'I need to wee.'

'Well, go outside and do it, you lunatic, if you're that bothered.'

I exited the barn. There was no one else around. I walked some distance away to relieve my bladder up a tree. It was a long wee. I'd just put my willy back in my trousers when I heard the first short scream – 'Ow!' – quickly followed by another. By the time I ran back to the barn, Katy's yelps of pain had turned to crying and pleading.

Cory had pulled up a nettle branch by the stem and was whipping his sister's bare arms and legs with it. She was hunched against a dusty brick wall in a foetal position, tucking her head in, trying to protect her face. Her arms were already coming out in a fearsome rash. I pulled the hammer from my waistband and ran up behind Cory to get him off her.

It was only a light hammer, good for little more than knocking in panel pins, so I swung it hard and aimed for the temple, which I knew was a weak spot. On that first blow he tried to turn and twist his shirt from my grip but his legs stayed where they were, folding him into a cross-legged sitting position, like an efficient bit of origami.

I told Katy to run and she took off without looking back.

Cory's eyes were looking in different directions, one up at me as if to say *what are you doing?*, the other gazing aimlessly at the sky outside. I thought he might stand up and come at me so I pushed him over onto his back with my foot then squatted next to him and hit him again in his upturned face.

The blunt end of the hammer went into his eye with a squishy sound that I've never forgotten. After that he lay subdued. His breath rattled, struggling to move in and out. I didn't stick around. I took one good look at what I had done to his face, dropped the hammer, then turned and ran.

I'm thinking about all this as I ride across the island, back to confront Laura with what I believe is the truth of who she is. Another storm has blown in and the rain is lashing into my face, but I keep turning the throttle and don't feel a damn thing.

Because I took the hammer with me that day, I was tried for murder, the prosecution arguing that it signalled a premeditated act. The second hammer blow, to Cory's eye socket, when he was already disabled, effectively sealed the charge as murder rather than manslaughter. It also meant that I could legally be named in the press, even though I was only twelve, only a child.

The trial was lengthy and sporadic, with a lot of psychological tests and evaluations before and in between, and as a 'continuing story' it drew national media interest. But that coverage was nothing compared with what it ballooned up to after they found out about my parents.

The village must have been crawling with reporters in my incarcerated absence, and you know what village gossip is like. One of the tabloids got hold of the story that my parents had been involved for some time in a sort of *ménage à quatre* with Cory's parents; swapping partners, staging their own private little orgies, watching each other fuck. Soon, all the papers had it.

Eventually, some of the details emerged in court, which is where I found out that the rumours other inmates had been mercilessly ribbing me about were all true, even as I was denying them as filthy lies; even though they so neatly explained why Cory's parents and mine wanted us out of the house so much, and why they were so keen for Cory and me to stay friends.

Cory's character also came under analysis in the trial, and, under oath, his mother and father were forced to testify to his having been a 'difficult child', sometimes prone to 'stubbornness' and acts of 'peevishness'; but they averred that he had never been in trouble at school or with the law and had never bullied his little sister. Cross-examined, they each admitted that Katy came home alone that day distressed and with her arms covered in severe nettle rash. But when they asked her what had happened she wouldn't say. They put it down to childish misadventure and soon forgot about it in the turmoil of their son being missing.

Maybe Cory's mum and dad agreed to lie in court about that to protect their son's squeaky-clean image. But it cut me up for years, believing that Katy didn't tell anyone what Cory did to her and what he was really like, when to do so might have helped me.

Looking back, I think the hammer would have still done for me. And I suppose Katy was scared and confused. After my trial was over and her parents saw me sentenced, the family moved away from the village, I never knew where to.

I couldn't blame her for not seeing the importance of getting the truth heard. She was only very young back then and probably severely traumatised.

But that was twenty-five years ago and she isn't that little girl any more.

Thirty-four

I pound on the door of Laura's hut in the throwing-down rain. It takes her a moment to open it.

'Mike.'

'My name's not Mike, and I think you know that.'

She steps aside. 'You'd better come in. Jesus, you're soaked through.'

'Never mind about that.' I shut the door behind me but the noise of the rain continues to clatter on the roof. 'I'm not Mike and you're not Laura.'

'What are you talking about? Is this some weird joke?'

'Oh, will you *stop* playing games, *please*?'

'O-kay.' She goes as still as a cobra facing a mongoose. 'Can we at least sit down?'

I take the chair by the table, dumping myself unceremoniously and very wetly on the clothes that are draped over it, and she sits down gingerly on the edge of the bed.

'How do you know Nick Davenport?' I ask her.

'What?'

I repeat the question.

'I've told you. We were partners. We lived together.'

'Yeah, and you still work together and you both got sent out to this conference and— *bullshit!*'

She looks startled. I give myself a second to calm the fuck down, which is what her expression is begging me to do.

'I've spoken with Nick Davenport. I don't know how you know him, but he certainly doesn't know you.'

'But at the bar on the junction. We saw him, together. You were there with me.'

'We saw someone. You pointed someone out in the crowd, but I didn't see him recognise you.'

'Because I was hiding, remember? Mike, what is all this? Is this about what happened between us last night and what I said about Nick?'

I ignore her attempt at diversion.

'You could have pointed to any passing stranger who looked like the professor type, and made the rest up from there. Except you knew his name. I don't know how, yet, but you knew his fucking name.'

'Mike, have you been following me? Spying on me or something?'

I reach into my satchel and pull out my dampened copy of the conference programme. At least she recognises what it is.

'You're not in there. You were never a delegate. You lied to me. So, of course, that raised some questions. And I started asking them.'

Laura stares down at the programme on the floor where I've tossed it and twists her lips as good as Shirley Bassey, searching for a way to hold off the inevitable aria of confession for a few more seconds.

'Laura, who are you?' I say gently, coaxing her to give it up, for her own sake as much as mine. 'You know who I am, don't you?'

She looks in my eyes and for a split second I see it again. That fear. Of me.

'I'm Steven Elwood,' I state. 'That's my real name. You know that name, don't you?'

I can see that she does but I want to hear her say it. She stays silent, frozen, cautious.

'You know it because you know me. We grew up together, didn't we? In the same village. In the same street. You were called Katy then. Maybe you had a middle name and maybe it was Laura. If so, I never knew. But you were called Katy Stewart. Was that your maiden name? Before Duxton.'

Laura continues to say nothing. She's like one of those psychoanalysts who don't even bother to repeat anything, just sit and wait for the client to go on filling the silence.

'So I'm Steven Elwood and you're Katy Stewart. The sister of Cory. The boy I killed when I was twelve. And I just want to know why you're here.'

'Mike. Steven. Stop, please. I'm not—'

'Hey You!'

We're interrupted by Lily's voice heading up a commotion outside which has just become audible under the noise of the downpour. We both jump at the bang of Laura's door flying open, followed by a police boot. Two cops, weapons thankfully holstered, march in and grab me by the arms, pulling me to my feet.

'What the fuck—?'

'You come with us, bring passport!' one of them yaps at me in English. Then he looks at Laura and points. 'And you. You come too. Bring passport.'

'What's this about?' I say, but get no answer from either of them, just 'Get passport! Come now!'.

Lily is busy berating the two young policemen from the porch in their own language, probably about the damage to the door, but they ignore whatever it is she's saying to them. They give Laura and me exactly one minute to get our shit together. Then one of them takes hold of Laura's arm while the other drags me out into the rain.

Thirty-five

The cell in the basement of the police station isn't pleasant when they dump me in it after relieving me of my passport, wristwatch and mobile phone, and it doesn't improve any in the twenty-four hours they keep me locked in there, during which no one questions me or tells me why I've been arrested.

The only ventilation is a barred, foot-wide window so high up and recessed in the back wall that we can't even see the sky through it without standing on one another's shoulders. The only view is the blank, whitewashed, facing brick wall and the stone floor of the passage outside the old-fashioned cell bars in the front. The walls of the cell run with reeking moisture – a precipitation of humidity, human sweat and the vapours of the slop bucket in the corner – and the floor runs with cockroaches.

There are three of us in the cell. There were two young locals already in here when they put me in, then they took one out and put another one in and the same thing happened again later. Three to a cell seems the strict norm. There are four cells on this corridor and there are three other prisoners in the cell next to ours while the other two cells stand empty. I admire their efficiency: they only have to maintain two cells instead of three or four.

This maintenance consists of the station's only policewoman being sent down once a day to slop out the buckets. And, as little as she seems to care for this duty, I'd still rather watch the poor woman only have to slop out two buckets instead of four.

To be honest, if the detainees were more evenly distributed it would make little difference to us. It's not like we're fighting over beds: there's the concrete floor and a blanket each, grubby from the turnover of previous occupants; thankfully no lice, so they must get washed from time to time, probably by the same long-suffering policewoman.

The cell is big enough for three of us to lie down together without touching in the night, and I have nothing which I need worry about being stolen except my dignity. I pass a stinking, sweat-soaked, mosquito-bitten night using one arm for a pillow and flapping cockroaches away with the other. Not much sleep gets slept by anyone, but then I never expected this place to be the Hilton. I just never expected to ever be a guest.

In the waking hours, we occupy a corner each, avoiding the bucket corner, and we sit and meditate, twiddle our thumbs and stamp on roaches, whose corpses are then removed piecemeal by a two-way column of ants. Occasionally we talk. I try to use their language and they try to use mine, and together we muddle through. We can communicate with the guys in the next cell even though we can't see them.

No one comes and tells us to shut up or anything. A cop, accompanied by another cop who is armed and standing at a short distance, brings us stainless-steel dishes of food a couple of times a day, some rice topped with a black goo that tastes of nothing, and there is the occasional removal or addition of a prisoner. Otherwise, we're left alone, as ignored and forgotten as a clapped-out old donkey.

Out of the prisoners that pass through while I'm there, three of them were picked up by the cops for possession of methamphetamine. In the night I hear the one in my cell, his teeth chattering; in the day he looks sweaty, aching and restless, but so do we all. At least we're not thirsty, they give us water. Probably tap water. No illness yet.

Another is here for some petty offence that I don't quite follow, even when my cellmates try to explain it to me in English. He is the only Muslim among us. I don't know how he knows which way Mecca is but he bends over and whispers his prayers at appropriate intervals of his body clock. The others are all Buddhists, I assume, and follow no religious observances during their stay, but they tolerate his without comment. Is it my imagination or does he make them nervous?

A couple of guys are traders like myself, thrown in here purely to be inconvenienced because they were late in paying off Bandura.

I am the only one among them who can't give an explanation for why he is here, and that, coupled with my foreignness, makes everyone else naturally a little suspicious of me. Maybe they think I'm a plant, a foreigner so desperate or compromised that he's willing to be a police spy. So I keep a cool head and don't ask any awkward questions and stay quiet a lot, ranging over my own thoughts.

Luckily, there are no hard-cases or nut-jobs in with us; we all just want to wait it out patiently, and with no trouble, until they come and get us; then, one way or another, we can get on with the rest of our lives.

Thirty-six

Contrary to any preconceptions of local tardiness, it's almost exactly twenty-four hours after first caging me up that they come and get me, though I only work this out later when I get back my Timex, evidently deemed too worthless for the police to bother keeping.

Two constables haul me up to Bandura's office and sit me down in front of his desk. The ceiling fan and the ever-present hum of sweat and cigarettes are refreshing after the foul odour and the wet buzzing heat of the cell. I notice they haven't handcuffed me. They can obviously tell that I'm no Jackie Chan escape artist but it may signal something else, so I try to stay alert. I don't want to become the prisoner who is 'shot while attempting to flee custody'. I let myself relax a little when Bandura looks up from his 'paperwork' and dismisses the two armed constables from the room.

'What did you do with Miss Duxton?' I ask immediately.

Bandura waves a hand. 'Miss Duxton is gone. We found no reason to detain her. She was released after an hour.'

That's the main thing off my mind. But I still don't know why I'm here. Until Bandura slides something across the desk.

'Explain these.'

I see the photographic contact strip of my headshots that I left on Panda's work desk and meant to go back for. I guess I left that too late.

'Passport photos,' I say. 'For when it runs out.'

Bandura pulls out my passport as if from thin air and opens it up.

'It doesn't run out for two more years.'

I can't think of a flip response, and, anyway, it would probably be unwise to make light of this right now.

'Captain Bandura, what is this about, exactly?'

154

Like a conjuror, he holds up the forged press pass in his other hand and lays it down on the desk, facing me. *Is that your card?* I know for certain then that they have searched my hut and taken anything they liked. Fortunately, anything else of importance lives in my satchel, and I left that in Laura's hut. I can only hope they didn't go back there.

'We know that you've been asking questions at Shiri Palace, pretending to be this Robert Lorrimer. We know you gained access to one of the bedrooms there. What were you doing? Casing the joint for a burglary?'

His badly-dubbed colloquialism is quaint but I think I can see where this is going.

'No,' I say. 'The truth is, I was there researching a book.'

Bandura taps the pass irritably.

'We received a complaint from one of the conference delegates.'

Fucking Davenport. Or Kristina?

'This alone is a serious offence,' he goes on, his finger poking my face on the pass. 'Impersonation, forgery.'

I almost say '*I* didn't forge it', but just in time I think of Panda. Maybe they have him here too and I don't want to snitch or give Bandura any more leverage over me than he already has.

'Am I under arrest? Because no one's taken my mugshot or fingerprinted me yet.'

A reptilian grin spreads beneath Bandura's moustache, which in turn rides up like an exotic caterpillar.

'I looked you up – Steven Elwood,' he reads off my passport. 'I know who you are. Saw many stories and YouTube videos. You are infamous. You were a bad boy.'

'And I did my time for it in *my own country*.' There's a phrase I never thought I'd hear myself using again with any conviction.

Bandura looks at me for a long time. I should be avoiding his alpha male glare right now but my eye is drawn to a fly that lands on his forehead and creeps around unnoticed, sucking at droplets of sweat.

'Two thousand dollars,' he says at last, leaning back. At his movement, the fly jumps ship. 'Make all this go away.'

'I don't have two thousand dollars.'

'But you have a bank account. Here in town.'

Shit.

'My—' I can barely bring myself to say it. 'My mother controls that account. It's for emergencies.'

'And what do you call this?'

He has a point I can't argue with.

'I'll have to call her.'

If he'd used a third hand to pull out my phone it wouldn't have surprised me. He pushes it across his desk.

'Then make the call.'

'What time is it?'

'Now, one o'clock p.m.'

'That means it's six in the morning there.'

'Good. Then she knows it's an emergency.'

I pick up the phone and check my credit.

'I don't have enough minutes left. It's a long distance call. I won't have enough time.'

Bandura eyes me suspiciously but doesn't check my phone to see if I'm lying, which I'm not. He leans across his desk and moves his landline phone towards me.

'Can I at least have some privacy, please?'

Bandura does something I've never seen him do before: he stands up from behind his desk and crosses the room. He is wearing trousers that match his tunic's gold piping and are in need of a pressing. He opens the door. A blank-faced constable enters and is told to keep watch over me. Then Bandura leaves me to my phone call, the cost of which he will no doubt add to my final bill.

Thirty-seven

Since my dad's death, a few years ago, I doubt that my mother has become an early riser. Even when she was still hairdressing, back in the day, she never set an appointment before ten. I try to picture her asleep in a bedroom I've never seen. I envisage her mobile phone next to the bed. I hear the tone that tells me it is ringing seven thousand miles away. I imagine it vibrating and moving on the nightstand, crawling around like that fly on Bandura's face. I almost give in to despair but it goes on ringing long enough for her to wake up and answer it.

'Hello?'

'Hello, Mum. It's Steven.'

There is a significant pause. Then:

'What do you want? Do you know what time it is?'

'I'm sorry. I wouldn't call if I didn't have to.'

I hear her sigh down the line.

'What is it, Steven?'

I know there is no room for pleasantries between us, and that neither of us wants or expects them.

'I need to make a withdrawal from the bank.'

'Again?'

'It's quite a large one. Two thousand dollars.'

I cast a glance at the constable by the door; he is looking intently, eyes forward, at a precise spot on the empty wall ahead.

'What's that in pounds?' says my mother.

'I'm not sure. About eighteen hundred, I think.'

'Bloody hell, Steven. Are you in trouble again?'

Again. The only other time she ever knew me to be in trouble was when I was twelve. But, *again.* Like it was just yesterday. Bitch.

'I will be if I don't get the money.'

'Where are you? No. Don't answer that. I don't want to know.' She sounds tired, more than just sleepy. 'Okay. I'll sort it out. But it won't be straight away. I'll have to call the bank when they open.'

'Mum,' I say, 'do it straight away as soon as they open. Please. It's urgent.'

'I'll do it as soon as I can,' she says impatiently. 'You've woken me up so I won't get back to sleep now, anyway.'

I grit my teeth.

'Thanks, Mum. It really is very important. Can you ring me when it's done?'

'Ring where?'

'My mobile. You've got the number. It's in your phone, remember?'

'Of course I remember, I'm not senile.'

'And, Mum. If someone else answers, just tell them "It's done". That's all. They'll know what you mean.'

'You haven't been kidnapped, have you? Steven – '

For a moment, she sounds like she might care.

'No, Mum. It's nothing like that, honest.'

'All right. But don't call me at this time again.' Her voice hardens a little more. 'In fact, don't call me at all if you don't have to.'

'Don't worry, Mum. I won't.'

I put the phone down on its cradle and the cop at the door calls Captain Bandura back in.

'It'll take three or four hours,' I say to the captain. 'She's going to call my mobile when it's authorised. I'll need to keep it on me.'

'No. I keep it.'

'Then you'll need to answer the call. If she asks you any questions, just hang up, will you? As long as she says it's done. Then I'll have to go to the bank.'

'Bank closes three-thirty. Not open again till tomorrow, eight-thirty.'

Shit. I don't know what to say. There's no other way I can do this. It's not like I own a cashpoint card and I doubt Bandura would take a cheque even if I could produce one.

Bandura resumes his seat and glares at me across the desk like a shark eyeing up its dinner.

'I don't like you in my town. To me, you are nothing but *farang*. But now you are troublemaker, too. First you pay the two thousand dollars. Make all this go away. Like a fresh start for you. But to continue to operate here, you now pay me twenty percent.'

I feel like the walls are closing in, squeezing off any way forward. All I can do is nod acceptance.

'What now?' I say. 'There's no way I can get you the money until tomorrow.'

'Now? Back to cells. I tell you when your mommy calls.'

They take me back downstairs. The guys in the cell have kept my corner warm for me. I sit down and contemplate the uncomfortable twenty-hour wait ahead of me for the bank to open in the morning.

But less than an hour later they come back and let me out. They lead me upstairs to the processing desk, where the only processing is for them to return my watch, phone and passport before letting me go. There is no paperwork to bother Bandura or the judicial system with. My incarceration never officially occurred.

Lily is waiting for me inside the police station doorway. She doesn't look happy.

'Jesus, Lily,' I say as we exit the station together. 'Did you pay off Bandura for me?'

She doesn't look at me, marching away quickly. 'Not me. Your lady friend.'

'Who, Laura?'

She doesn't confirm it, just huffs as I begin following her back to Lily's Beach Huts.

'Is she still here?' I ask.

Lily still won't look at me. 'She gone.'

I trot at Lily's shoulder as she zips along at a pace my cramped and stiff limbs can barely keep up with. She is really not happy with me at all. I know that whatever happens next is going to be bad.

Thirty-eight

Back at the huts, I ask Lily if she's cleaned Laura's hut since she departed.

'Yes, I clean. Got new guest already.'

'Did you find my bag in there?'

Lily speaks in a quiet, level, empty voice: 'Come inside the house.'

I follow her through to the small, sparsely-furnished parlour at the front of the house, where a grimy mosquito-screened window looks dimly out onto the strip. Lily bends over and reaches with both hands inside a varnished dark-wood sideboard. She stands up and stretches out one arm holding my satchel by its strap.

I take hold of the strap. She stares at me balefully but she doesn't let go, and I know what is coming. She tugs it back, pulling me off balance, and her other arm rises up, clutching one end of a three-foot bamboo cane. She brings it down first on the hand holding the satchel, the force of it palpable as the cane whistles past my ear. The back of my hand goes numb then burns fiercely and I pull it away, letting the satchel drop to the floor and yelping like Katy Stewart when Cory whipped her with nettles.

'Fuck!'

She doesn't let me nurse it. That was just the start. A second switch of the cane slashes my thigh. A third cracks me across the arm on the same side as I raise it to protect myself. I twist in agony and hop back from the cane's reach but the room is too small and I crash into something. I tumble over the edge of an armchair and wind up on the floor. That's when Lily steps in and really goes to work on me.

I take most of the upper-body blows on my arms and shoulders, keeping my face and head shielded. I kick my legs out at her to defend my lower body but whack after whack sears into me across my bare thighs, shins and ankles. Every place the cane slashes me feels like it is branded with a hot poker. I cry out for her to stop but I know she won't. Not till she's done. Not till she hears the cane crack and split, and witnesses the blood and tears of my contrition.

The stupid thing is, if I wanted to, I could grab the cane and wrench it from her hand. I could stand up and put a stop to this immediately. Lily is nothing but a short, overweight, middle-aged woman who smokes too much. I could take hold of that walnut of a head and ram it through the flimsy plasterboard wall if I wanted to, and there'd be nothing she could do about it.

But I don't. I take the beating.

I take the beating because Lily took me in. I take the beating because Lily put a roof over my head. I take the beating because Lily serves me breakfast. I take the beating because Lily used her seniority to smooth things over with the local community so I could set up in business. I take the beating because Lily praises me when I do good and punishes me when I do bad, and treats me like her own kin. I take the beating because Lily has the right to give me it.

And I take the beating because I deserve it.

When it finally stops, Lily straightens her back laboriously, takes a backward step and returns the broken cane to the sideboard cupboard. It's a ritual I've witnessed before from this same position. For every new beating, a new cane emerges from the cupboard. Before she can turn and look down at me with that baleful stare which always follows, I grab my satchel and drag it back through the house on my hands and knees.

At the back door jamb, I pull myself up to my feet and stagger out into the garden. A couple of young blokes – shorts, flip-flops, baseball caps, tattoos – are walking up from the huts. They see me and quicken their pace.

'Fuckin'ell, you all right, mate?'

I shield myself from their helping hands before they can put them on me. They might burn themselves on my skin.

'Yeah, yeah. I'm okay. I'll be fine.'

'D'you want us to fetch a doctor or something?' This one's accent is Australian.

'No. No doctors. I've got someone who'll look after me.'

'I dunno, mate, you look pretty fuckin' banged up.' He looks at the stripes of bleeding flesh on my arms and legs. 'What the fuck happened?'

'I fell off my bike. Really. Please. I'm all right. Nothing's broken. I just need to get to the hut.'

They support me in the back and under my armpits, places Lily's rod didn't get to, and I crook my arms over their shoulders and they help me hobble back to my door. I groan my appreciation and as they turn away I shut the door, drop the bag on the floor and lower myself carefully onto the bed.

Thirty-nine

In Singapore the authorities would've had to give me a medical examination first to show I was fit enough to take a caning like that. In Singapore, there are no canings like that. For an hour I am too weak and in pain to do anything but lie curled up on the bed on my less-wounded side, trying not to touch my sizzling flesh. When this becomes intolerable, I roll over on to my back and wince at the inflamed sores across my shoulders. The skin of my limbs burns so intensely that the room begins to feel cold. I feel like I'm wrapped in the arms of a stinging jellyfish.

Eventually, I realise that I need to stand up and clean these wounds before they get infected. I struggle in the bathroom for a crippling half hour with the *mandi*, washing off the blood, scrubbing the wounds as hard as I can bear for fear of leaving them dirty, and rinsing off with the clean water in the tank. The habitually lukewarm water feels icy on my skin. I carefully pat myself dry with a clean towel then get back into bed, pulling a sheet over my naked trembling body, and I stay there like that for a week.

Towards sundown that first day, I hear my mobile ring but I don't even try to get to it. My mother returning my call from the police station – probably leaving a message that will ping off into the ether some place where I'll never hear it back: *It's done.*

I realise I'm shivering and burning up all over at the same time. I know it's probably a fever but my muscles are too locked for me to get up and do anything about it. I shake and contract like that, my mind speeding and distorting, until it turns completely dark, both outside and in. I can't spend a night like this, I'll go batshit.

Soon after, I hear the door open and see a warm, fuzzy light enter the room, like a giant firefly. As my eyes adjust, it becomes an oil lamp, not floating but held aloft by Lily. The lady of the lamp. She steps inside, closes the door and places the lamp on the table, from where it throws a consoling corona over my sad little room.

I try to look Lily in the eye but I can't stop shaking. Her face quivers and judders in the lamplight. She is gazing down at me with what looks like compassion. Then tears spring to my eyes and her face shimmers out of vision altogether.

'You let Lily disinfect those cuts,' she says.

She leans over the bed and moves the sheet to uncover first my torso, then my legs up to the hip. As she does this, she takes care to lift the sheet clear of my skin so as not to let the material graze against me. Then she sits down next to me on the bed, produces a tub of antiseptic cream and a supply of cotton-wool buds, and spends the next hour treating the damage she inflicted on me. We don't talk, other than the odd 'turn over' or 'move that arm'. I let her do what she needs to do and try to suffer it without whimpering.

When it's over, she holds out a small brown medicine bottle.

'Here. Antibiotics.'

'Not yet,' I say. 'Let's wait and see.'

She goes away, leaving me the lamp, and comes back after ten minutes with some ginseng tea.

'You drink this.'

I prop myself up, though it costs me agony, and sip some of the brew. She leaves it for me on the floor by the bed.

'You want fan?'

I don't know. I don't know what I want.

She switches it on anyway, then goes away and leaves me alone.

Forty

For the next seven days, the only time I get out of that bed is to struggle to the toilet. Otherwise, I lie there, sometimes dozing, sometimes awake, mostly something in between, cooking in a mesmeric cauldron of pain.

Lily's frequent visits to my bedside come to define the pattern of the days as she nurses the fever out of my system. Once I am out of the woods, she feeds me, plumps up my pillow, brings me herbal remedies for my recovery and soothing oils for my smarting skin. When I feel I'm up to it, she bed-baths me and gently helps me to roll this way and that so that she can change the sheets.

'Keep sheets clean and smooth from now on. And no eating in bed! You eat over edge of bed. Don't want crumbs to make bedsores.'

Once I can manage the pain, I am able to prop up and read my copy of *The Quiet American*. It's a sad tale of cynical old age pitted against misplaced youthful idealism, competing for a delicate but hardy Oriental flower, and ultimately it offers no parallels at all with me and Laura. The book inevitably makes me think of her, but the pain soon drives those thoughts away. Until I'm ready to face them.

After a week on my back, I sleep more easily and for longer stretches, thus aiding the body's recovery, and in my waking hours I'm finally able to stay sitting up without wanting to curl up into a ball. The pain is still very much present but all the underlying bruising has come out, making it more generalised and less like an ongoing shark attack. My arms and legs look like I've been sucked through a ship's propeller blades. I'm stiff as a board at first, but once my mobility begins to return it improves quite rapidly.

I check the room properly for the first time since my convalescence and the only things I see missing are the bottle of rum that I'd opened and the remainder of the vodka that I plied Pieter Visser with. Nothing else was of enough interest or value to tempt the police. Then my forgotten satchel catches my eye, slung by Lily over the back of a chair. Everything I left in the satchel is still there. My ID card, my binoculars, the Maglite, my wallet, the bit of cash contained in it. My notebook and pen. Even the wrinkled conference programme, which someone picked up off the floor and replaced. It's all there. Laura protected it for me. At least she could be trusted to do that. Laura protected it from the police for me and Lily kept it safe.

I finally feel up to thinking about her. About Laura. And about the last thing she said to me before we were separated by the police:

I'm not—

It seems obvious from the context what she was about to say: *I'm not who you think I am. I'm not Katy Stewart.* But I can't be sure. In fact, there's still damn little I can be sure of. I still believe that Laura never met Nick Davenport but she neither confirmed nor denied it. Yet how did she put the right name to the face that walked past us in the street that day? Will I ever know the answer to that? The only thing I'm sure of is that I can't be sure of anything any more.

Fragments of such thoughts tormented my fever-swirled head for long days in which I was incapable of creating any order out of them; but even now that I can, their only effect is to frustrate me. They go round in circles, questions seeking answers that will never come; not now that Laura is gone.

I turn my mind to Panda and the trouble he must be in. For Bandura to get hold of those photos of me, the police must have raided his shack, and since then it's been what – eight days, nine? They won't have kept him in the relative luxury of a police cell all that time. He could be stuffed away in any hole of detention by now. The prison on the island, or even one over on the mainland somewhere. I have no idea which district's jurisdiction we are in, never having had cause to think about it before.

I wonder if anyone is looking after his shack or feeding the chickens in the yard, and whether my body is up to riding up there yet to find out. I test myself by going outside and walking a few paces but I tire quickly, fighting the soreness and stiffness in the cloying heat, and as soon as sunlight touches my skin the old burning sensation stokes up and I have to retreat back into the shadows of my room.

Lily continues to treat my wounds with special oils that she gets from who knows where, and which bring me some relief. The wounds have scabbed over now. I just have to resist picking the scabs, or scratching them when they itch. The oils help with that too. I lie on the bed with the sheet covering my modesty and she applies them tenderly with hands that feel surprisingly soft. Other than simple instructions, we don't talk. It's the same when she feeds me or brings me her herbal teas. We say only what is necessary or polite. She ignores the various elephants in the room and I take my cue from her.

Every day the pain lessens and becomes more manageable. Every day I feel a bit more of my strength returning. Very soon, now, I'll be able to go back out into the world and find out how much of my old life is left.

Forty-one

It's on a hot, bright, clear mid-morning two weeks after my 'arrest' that I pull the bike up outside Panda's shack. The yellow butterflies are gambolling and the shady glade is filled with twittering birdsong and echoing with the squawks of parakeets. No one is around. Panda's paintings have been removed from the veranda and the shack looks closed up.

I knock on the door and call Panda's name. After a while, I detect movement inside. The door unlatches and Panda stands there filling the frame, larger than life and twice as beautiful.

'Fucking hell,' I say, 'I thought you must have been taken away by the cops.'

'I know, brother. Bad times, bad times.'

We hug and then unclench when I flinch.

'You okay, bro?' He looks at my long cotton sleeves and trousers that cover the welts and bruises.

'Yeah, I'm good.'

He steps outside to join me in the yard, and I sense that something's off immediately. Panda paces around anxiously, not settling in one spot, running a hand through his hair again and again and avoiding eye contact with me.

'Did they take you in as well?' I ask him.

'Who, bro?'

'The cops. They had me locked up for a whole day and night. Had to pay off fucking Bandura big time.'

I don't tell him someone else paid. That part is none of Panda's business and from now on he is best kept out of it.

'Mm. Bandura. Yeah,' is all he says.

'What's wrong?' I ask.

'I'm sorry, bro. I wasn't expecting him to show up unannounced.'

'Who?'

169

'Fucking Bandura, man.' Panda is animated now, throwing his arms about. 'Took me by surprise before I could destroy those shots. He just picked them up off the desk before I could do anything about it. Knew your face straight away.'

For a moment, I don't understand. Then I begin to understand.

'Bandura was here?' I'm still trying not to understand, hoping for an innocent explanation. 'I don't get it. Bandura never leaves his office.'

'I'm sorry, bro,' Panda repeats. 'It wasn't supposed to go down like that.'

I try to imagine what was going down, and how it was supposed to go down, and I don't like the picture I'm coming up with.

'Were you—? Are you—?'

The look of shame on Panda's face is all the answer I need. I propel myself across the distance he's put between us and although he can see it coming it's too late, I land a punch to the jaw that puts him on his fat arse on the ground.

'You're a fucking snitch?' I whimper at him. 'I don't believe this. You're in Bandura's pocket!'

Panda reaches for his glasses on the ground, wipes them on his T-shirt and hooks them back on to his face. For a long time I stand over him ready to punch him again if he tries to deny it. But Panda remains sitting quietly in the dust, his forearm balanced on his knee as he stares miserably at the dirt. After a while, he looks up at me and I reach out a hand to help him to his feet.

'Bandura got his claws into me just like he got them into you and everyone else, bro. How else do you think I keep this place going? He comes up here in person to take his cut because I can't be seen going to him. It's a private arrangement. Only, instead of money, he wants information.'

'And whose idea was that?'

'His, man, his. If I don't play his game he'll shut me down and lock me up for good. But it was never about you, brother. I would never sell you out. I thought you'd taken those photos with you, like we agreed. I didn't know they were still on the desk until it was too late. Honest, bro, you have to believe me. I would never sell you out.'

I do believe him but it doesn't make the betrayal of trust any easier to accept. Panda has just given me a secret that I never asked for and it becomes another lie for me to have to maintain. I thought I'd finished with lies after Laura departed. They were lies I got myself into, lies I could have been imprisoned for, and that's why Lily did what she felt she had to do to teach me a lesson. If I take on another lie, even though it is someone else's, then my punishment will have been for nothing.

Of course, I can simply keep my mouth shut. What doesn't come out of it can't be a lie. But suppose I'm not the only one who knows, or suspects, Panda's 'arrangement' with Bandura. If anyone asks me about him, if any bad people in town, for instance, were to express doubts about his trustworthiness, either through Lily or to me directly, what else can I do but lie? I thought I loved Panda. I do love him. But I don't have the stomach for this any more. And it's as if he can read my thoughts:

'You gotta keep this between us, bro. You tell the wrong people, I'm dead, brother, you know it.'

I look at him standing there, a man with a good twenty kilos in weight and ten centimetres in height on me, and you know what I think? If the big klutz had a single scheming self-serving impulse in his body, he would do me in to shut me up right now, then phone his buddy Bandura to come and dispose of the corpse. Instead, he looks terrified.

I reach out and he flinches, but I rest my hand softly on his shoulder in reassurance and apology.

'I'm sorry, mate,' I say. 'I shouldn't have done that. I guess you've got to hustle to Bandura's tune just like the rest of us. There's no reason why you should be a saint.'

'You know you're my good friend, bro, always.' He puts his hand to his heart. 'I didn't tell Bandura's ass nothing about you. You feel me?'

'I know, don't worry.'

I know Bandura found his own window into my lurid background without any help from Panda, and I tell him what I told Visser, but this time with feeling:

'Your secret's safe with me.'

'Did the cops do that to you?'

'What?'

He gestures at me. 'You're hurting, bro, an' covering up.'

'It wasn't the cops.' I wait a couple of beats, then say: 'It was Lily.'

'Oh.' He understands. 'Hey, you can't say anything about this to Lily, right? She crosses paths with some serious people, you know?'

'I do. I won't tell a soul. I promise.'

How can I not promise? He has kept the secret of my identity for the last five years. I owe him the same obligation. But, of course, the lesson I take away from this episode is the same one I've been relearning for most of my miserable life in this vile world. Trust no one. In the end, they all let you down. In fact, don't even trust yourself. Because, if it ever comes to the crunch between keeping Panda's secret and saving my own skin, I can't be trusted to stick to my promise. I can only console myself with the knowledge that he must know that too. The only dead sure guarantee is if I take myself off somewhere where his secret is of no value to anyone.

How can anyone go on living like that in the world and have any hope of making a connection with another person? Is that a Catch-22? When to trust is the only way to know someone; someone who will only end up breaking your trust. If it isn't technically a Catch-22, it sure feels like it because the only loophole out of the conundrum is loneliness and isolation.

The only person who hasn't let me down in all this is Lily.

Forty-two

Lily stops taking care of me once she sees I am able to take care of myself again. I soon burn through my remaining cash, and I have to go back to work to survive. Bandura's twenty percent cripples me, especially after Lily puts the rent up for the beach huts to meet her own payoffs. I have to tout till four or five a.m. every night, and weekends off once more become a dream lost to the past. But I'm determined to see the season out just to spite the greedy xenophobic cop fuck. Then I'll make my move.

Bandura never said why he was raising his cut, or that there was a reason at all other than he can do whatever the hell he wants; but Lily's word proves prophetic, and soon everybody's tax goes up to fifteen percent as a blanket policy, the only exception, it seems, being me, the *farang* who pays twenty. Pretty soon, the word is going around all the snack bars and corners along the strip. Something's in the wind.

'Like what?' the conversation goes.

'Something big. Something national. The government is going to crack down again.'

'On what? Tourism? The economy would collapse.'

'Maybe not tourism. But immorality. There's a big Muslim population in the south. Terror attacks, sometimes. Maybe they put pressure on the government to clean up the drugs and the clubs. Maybe Bandura knows this is what's coming. Maybe he's building a retirement fund before the goose stops laying the golden eggs.'

'Bullshit. No one's going to close down the clubs. That's ridiculous. We'd all be fucked.'

I never contribute to the debate but I listen to the wind and I try to make my plans. My cover is blown here, it's time to move on. I know that Bandura will one day use his knowledge of my true identity against me if he thinks there's a way to make money from it. If he is planning his retirement, that day will come sooner rather than later. And if something bigger really is in the wind, either nearer or farther down the road, I don't want to stick around to see it.

I still haven't forgotten about the two thousand dollars my mother was going to authorise me to withdraw from the bank. If she left me a message, I never found it. I don't even know if it was her making the call I missed, but I can't think who else it might have been. If it was my mother, it means she was phoning to say it was done. All I can do is hope that she didn't undo it. But I'm in no hurry to find out. Not until the end of the season. If Bandura's spies see me going to the bank, he'll be ready to pounce because he won't have forgotten about that two thousand dollars either.

I'll have to sell my bike. That and the bank money should get me where I want to go. Except that I don't want to go anywhere. I like it here. Did. For a few years things were good. Quiet and tolerable. But I'm worried about what's to come, and that kind of worry is like the end of a love affair: once you start down that road there's no turning back.

Leave by boat. Work my passage. A private arrangement. Post no trail. Get out of the Gulf. Avoid the holiday islands. Get to Java. One of the cities. Jakarta or Yogya. Learn Bahasa. Easier than the language here. Get lost in the crowd. Start over again.

But I can't start over again. I'm approaching forty years old and I just don't have it in me any more. I think that it's when I reach this point that Lily intuits my despair and stops freezing me out.

One morning, she comes and knocks on my door. I'm already up and decently enough covered to open it straight away. She tilts back her head and looks me square in the eye, then speaks:

'Steven.'

She puts her hands together in the *namaste* prayer position and bows her head towards them. I instinctively return the gesture.

'You come now. Breakfast ready. Time for us to talk.'

I follow her up to the breakfast terrace. Everything is already laid out. Orange juice, croissants, the works. We sit down in the morning sunlight and Lily pours us both coffee. I lift a croissant from the plate and Lily smiles at me for the first time in weeks. Then she speaks.

'You good boy in your heart. I see that. But sometime you do wrong thing because you mixed up in here.' She pats herself on the head. 'Why you do wrong thing with that lady? It bring trouble not just for you. For me too.'

'I know,' I say. 'I'm sorry, Lily. I never meant to cause any trouble for you.'

'What that lady to you? Why she come here? Why she not stay Shiri Palace? Keep trouble up there.'

'She was never going to stay there. That was a lie. I don't know what she wanted. The police took me away before I could find out.'

'You think she come here for you?'

'Maybe.' I pause, sip my lukewarm coffee. 'For a while, I thought she was the sister of the boy I killed. I thought she'd come here to... I don't know. Pursue a grudge, maybe? Thank me? Perhaps even forgive me.'

Lily looks puzzled, maybe because I never gave her the full story before.

'Why she thank you for killing her brother?'

I look Lily carefully in the eye. 'Cory Stewart was a bad boy. Not just to me. To his sister as well. I had to stop him hurting her. I didn't have a choice.'

Lily gives me a doleful look, imagining a child's pain and confusion.

'Anyway,' I sail on, 'it probably wasn't her. I mean Laura. I don't believe she was the sister. Katy.'

The two names echo through my mind like ghosts in a forest.

'You like this girl, no?' says Lily sympathetically. 'You miss your Katy.' Then she turns her head and spits on the ground. 'Bandura ruin everything! I see it. You going to leave here. Move on some other place. I see it in your eyes.'

'It's time, Lily. We knew it would be, one day.'

We sit quietly for a while, eating our breakfast, listening to the birdsong and the distant soughing of the sea. Then Lily stands up and disappears inside for a moment. She comes back out and holds something out to me.

'Time you read this. Maybe it give you some answers.'

She hands me a sealed envelope with my handwritten name on the front: *Steven Elwood.*

'I keep it till she far away. In here.' She points to my chest where my heart should be. 'I think now time is right.'

I start to tear the flap of the envelope but Lily stops me.

'Not here. This just for you.'

Forty-three

I take the letter down to the beach and find a spot apart from all the sun-worshipping and beach massages where I sit on the verge among a pack of dogs in the shade of a palm grove. The dogs, in their slumber, ignore me as I open the envelope with trembling fingers. I pull out two A4 sheets and unfold a letter written in a neat hand. I take a deep breath and begin to read.

Dear Steven,
My name is Laura Duxton. That's my real name. In case you're still wondering, my maiden name was Fairchild. I don't know whether this will be a relief to you or a disappointment. I am not Katy Stewart. But I know who she is, and who you are.
As I'm pretty sure you suspected, I'm not an academic. My being here for the climate conference and my connection with Nicholas Davenport were a well-researched and improvised cover story intended for you. I'd like to be able to say I've never met Davenport, but actually I have. I interviewed him last year for a local newspaper about a book he'd just published, but I doubt that he would remember me or my name. Seeing him on the street with you outside the bar at the road junction was a lucky coincidence which I exploited to deepen my cover. So, essentially, I'm a journalist. Sorry. I like to think of myself more as a writer but that probably doesn't make you feel any better about my deception.
Six months ago I wrote an article about the Cory Stewart killing for <u>True Crime</u> magazine. The twenty-fifth anniversary of the incident was coming up, and the article, when it came out, attracted a boost in sales of that issue. So much so that the publishers proposed that I write a new book about the case. The fresh angle they wanted me to take was,

what has Steven Elwood been doing since he fell off the radar nearly ten years ago, and where is he now?

I was broke at the time, scraping by doing freelance work for little or no payment. The publishers were offering me a five-figure advance and a research budget. There was no way I could afford to turn it down. I really do live in Cambridge and it is not a cheap place to live.

My first move was to employ an investigator. It helped that she used to work for the police and was familiar with your case and those involved. She spoke with your mother, who was not helpful, but was unable to track down any of the Stewart family. She later managed to find out when you had left the country and in which direction you had gone. She was able to track your movements as far as Bali, but the trail went cold there, five years ago. So I got on a plane to Indonesia.

I kicked around Bali for a month trying to track down any leads I could find. I had plenty of pictures of you to show around but none more recent than from almost a decade ago. I finally found a bar owner who recognised you as someone he once employed. He said you hadn't changed much. He remembered you'd left Bali by boat, headed for the Gulf of Thailand. He even remembered the name of the vessel. After that, I trawled the docks until I found it, and spoke with the captain. It's amazing what people are able to dredge from their memories when a cash incentive is involved. From there I took a flight to your island.

I'll be honest, I didn't know what would happen once I found you. I didn't have a game plan. I just needed a way to get to know you. I booked into a hotel near the airport then scoped you out from a distance for a couple of days before making contact. Got to know what you did, where you hung out on the main strip, how to recognise your scooter. I thought it would be hard to find a way in that would enable our paths to continue crossing. So I contrived to hire you, thinking I could retain you for a week. I couldn't believe my luck when you installed me in the hut next to yours.

I knew that you hadn't been in any trouble with the law in the UK from the time of your release to your going into self-imposed exile, and my investigator found nothing to suggest that you had been in trouble anywhere else since. I'd also reviewed your trial, and felt that you'd been treated harshly considering the mitigating factors in the parental background. What I'm trying to say is that I knew I'd be safe with you. And I was. Well, until the police arrived, I guess.

I'm sorry I had to lie to you. If I'd told you the truth from the off, would you have let me in? I don't think so, and I wouldn't blame you. I'm also sorry if I appeared to lead you on romantically. That was not part of any game plan and it was not my intention. The truth is, I have a boyfriend at home, but the relationship is in decline, we don't make each other happy any more, and you were a sweet guy in a tropical paradise, and who knows what might have happened?

I am going to write the book, with or without your blessing. I hope it's with. I want the public to know the truth about what happened that day, and why. My investigator is still looking for Katy Stewart and I'm sure she'll find her. She doesn't give up easily. I just hope that, when she does, Katy will agree to talk with me. I think if the police hadn't arrived I might have got the truth from you. If you want to finish the conversation we started, you'll find my contact details at the end of this letter.

I know you want to stay out of the limelight and I respect that. I'd like to write about the man you are now, but people's names, locations, even occupations, can be disguised as you see fit. I'd even be happy for you to vet the book before it goes to the publisher if that is what you want. Any contributions from you would be financially rewarded, and incorporated anonymously if you so wished.

After the police released me, your friend Lily explained to me the bind you were in with the local police captain. She's a smart businesswoman and seems to have your best interests at heart. But I needed little persuasion from her, I thought the

179

*least I could do was let my publishers pay for your release.
You've spent more than enough time locked up already. I
hope you can still make a go of things here. Or if you move
on, perhaps we can stay in touch?*

*The police thing frightened me and I'm bolting back to
England like a coward. I'm sorry. I don't know why they
arrested you. Maybe I don't want to know, because I don't
want to think badly of you. What kind of a journalist does
that make me? But if I wait for you to get out of jail, I don't
know what I'll say to you that won't break your heart. I need
to take stock and recharge my batteries. But if you ever feel
like talking face to face again and giving me your side of the
story, I'm sure I could come back and we could pick up
where we left off.*

*Take care and all the best,
Laura x*

I look up and gaze at the sea. At least, now, I know. Who she
is. What she is. I don't know how I feel about it, but at least I
know.

My bloody mother! Why didn't she tell me someone had
been asking about me? She could have saved me a lot of
trouble and humiliation. I could have been ready, alert,
knowing a journalist might show up.

But, of course, it *did* occur to me that that's what Laura
might be. It occurred to me that time up at Shiri Palace when
I questioned the receptionist, but if I'm honest it occurred to
me from the word go, just as it always has done with any too-
friendly stranger ever since that Brit recognised me in the bar
in Kuta that time; the same bar where Laura picked up my
trail. But somewhere along the way I let myself think she
might be something else. Someone else.

There's got to be a huge dollop of irony in there
somewhere. She was a journalist pretending to be someone
else in order to stalk me, while I was someone else
pretending to be a journalist in order to stalk her. I guess

somewhere along the line we cancelled each other out quite neatly.

I take the letter up to my hut, then strip to my swimming shorts and go back down to the sea. I fix my sights on the raft, anchored out there beyond the white-tops, and slip into the water.

I regulate my breathing and swim with long, steady, confident strokes. When I reach the platform, I touch it with one hand, as if for luck, then turn around and head straight back to shore. When I walk out of the sea and up to my hut, my head is finally clear.

I sit out on the veranda with my notebook and pen. I read through everything I wrote there in pursuit of a story, this story, then go back and tear out those pages. I turn to a clean page and finally write the one true sentence I've been searching for all this time, and which was there all along:

'My name is Steven Elwood and I once killed a boy called Cory Stewart.'

Part Two
Gulf of Finland

Before the Gulf

Forty-four

This is my first winter in Helsinki.

The city is a land of spectacularly long shadows thrown by the low sub-Arctic sun onto bright surfaces of deep snow. The fluffy snow-coated fir trees; the tall but inviting apartment houses; the giant cruise liners, cities of the waves, anchored at the docks; the imposing Russian church across the harbour; the three-masted schooner permanently moored by the fish market, the sea reaching right up to the main square: all bask in a special light in winter, if only for a handful of hours a day.

The Finns are a friendly people who all speak perfect English and are the best-educated nation on earth. They can be gloomy at this time of year and seek solace in too much vodka. But they are a phlegmatic people, not easily given over to displays of strong emotion, and not much interested in salaciousness or sensationalism. Once I got my financial independence, it seemed like a good place to settle down. Quiet. Tolerant. Private.

I wrote the book longhand holed up in a shitty boarding-house in Yogyakarta, where I'd found bar work. And that's all I did. Work. Flat out, for a year. Tend bar, go home, write, sleep. Spend as little as possible. I found my perfect rhythm of self-denial. I needed this solitary existence for me to trawl through memories and feelings I thought I'd long since let go of. At the end, I had it finished: the official memoir that would trump Laura's book. The whole story, straight from the horse's mouth.

I knew from my mother that both of Cory's parents were now dead, killed together in a car accident on a motorway in France, where they'd moved to a cottage in the middle of nowhere. It meant that nothing I wrote or said or did from now on could hurt them any more. As for my mother, I didn't particularly care whether she felt hurt or not. She had a way of letting things bounce off her. She would either survive or she wouldn't.

That only left Katy to consider. If Laura ever found her (which I later learned that she did) she never let me know. An admirable case of a journalist protecting a source, maybe. Or perhaps she just respects my remoteness, since I've never contacted her. But I couldn't hang around until someone found Katy. I couldn't live the life I was living any longer, sweltering pointlessly in the stinking tropics feeling more like a fish out of water the older I got. I had to create at least the possibility of escape.

I went with a different publisher to Laura Duxton's. All it really took was my name for them to snap me up. They wanted somebody to ghostwrite it but I said no way and they soon backed down. The agent I subsequently took on said if I'd come to him first there would have been a bidding war. I'm glad I didn't. It would have been too tasteless and mercenary, maximising profit from a young boy's death. All I wanted was enough money to come back to Europe and get on with my life with some peace of mind. I wanted to show the world my true face before retreating to somewhere I could live openly as Steven Elwood without anyone caring who I was.

I titled the book *Bad Boy, Good Boy*. It was deliberately ambiguous. Did it refer to me and Cory, or to the person I was then and the person I am now? The 'public', meaning the media, took it as provocative, which helped sales no end. And the more my book sold, the more Laura's sold. The real public wanted to read both sides of the story, from the woman who met him and from the man himself. I don't begrudge her this success, she worked hard for it, though I've never read her book. I wonder if she's read mine.

Am I finally a writer? I don't know. There was a book in me that had to come out, but maybe that's it. What else do I write about that won't be self-referential? Since the book, I've written a few articles for a couple of quality European magazines that pay well and don't pester me for a face-to-face interview, and maybe I'm finally being accepted as Steven Elwood, writer, and not just The Boy Who Killed

Cory Stewart. I reject any invitations from the British tabloid press. I'm sure they can locate me if they want to, but they know they will get nothing from me.

My publishers want me to write a travel book, revisiting the sites of my nine-year flight from public attention. But I don't want to go back to those places. And I don't want to go back to the island. I miss Lily, and Panda, but when I start thinking that I miss Danny I realise I'm missing the past, a life that isn't there any more.

I was in Yogya when I heard about the bomb attack. It must have been about ten months after I left because the heavy tourist season had come round again. Eighteen people killed, most of them westerners, half of them Australians. The target was Copland, and if that suggested a link to Captain Bandura's wind of change I didn't want to know about it. Except maybe to hinge the plot of a novel on.

The police blamed the attack on southern Islamists. No surprises there. After that, tourism slumped, but the moral crackdown everyone was worrying about failed to manifest itself, and I thought the numbers would gradually pick up again. Then a young German backpacker got raped and murdered on the beach, the police blaming it on local Muslim fishermen. That kind of thing doesn't help. But these things go in circular phases – that's my philosophical take on it.

In the meantime, my take on the environment has become anything but philosophical. I've tried to channel some money to the right causes and I've bolstered the numbers at every Extinction Rebellion event I can get to without flying.

A few months after my settling in Helsinki, the university hosted a conference on the environment, and I discovered that one of the guest speakers was 'Professor' Pieter Visser of the University of Utrecht. I smiled when I saw that, imagining his pedantic ire at the misnomer which has perpetually dogged him. I didn't need a fake press pass this time, I got myself a real one from one of the magazines I contributed to. I was going to write a real report and everything.

I recognised Visser straight away. Out of bed, he stood a head taller than me. He was big and broad, and I thought again of all that weight falling twenty feet and hitting the slabs below the balcony at Shiri Palace. No traces of his injuries remained, however, and he looked trimmer than the last time I'd seen him, somehow, as if he might have quit drinking. When I sidled up to him in the refreshments area during an interval and said hello, he didn't recognise me, which was hardly surprising.

'I visited you in hospital after your accident at the ASEAN conference a couple of years ago.'

His eyes opened wide.

'My God. Yes, of course.' He racked his brains. 'Bob! The reporter who wasn't actually a reporter.'

'Actually, my real name's Steven – Steven Elwood.'

We shook hands and laughed over the serendipity of our meeting there. Then he started looking nervous for some reason.

'What are you doing here?' he asked me.

'I live here now.'

'In Finland?'

'Yeah. Weird, right?'

'Yes, that is weird. But what brings you to the conference?'

'I just thought I'd stop by and say hello. I'm covering it, actually. For *Paris Match*.' I showed him my press card. 'It's a real one this time.'

Visser looked suddenly relieved and more at ease with me.

'I'm so happy for you, my boy.' He gripped me by the shoulders. 'I was so worried I might have done something to ruin your career.' Then he froze, looked around and whispered in my face: 'You're not here to blackmail me over that balcony business, are you?'

'No! That was— Wait a minute! What do you mean, ruin my career?'

'My complaint. To the policeman. He came back to the hospital after I saw you. I told him I'd had a visitor bearing false credentials.' He shook his head. 'It was foolish of me at the time, I know. What is the correct word? Churlish. You told me the story was about someone else and I was feeling sorry for myself. Aggrieved, that's the word. I'm truly sorry if it caused you any inconvenience with the authorities.'

So it wasn't Davenport who'd dobbed me in: someone else I'd wronged, if only in thought. But as with my mother, I didn't care very much. I laughed the revelation off and told Visser there were no hard feelings and that I hoped my article would do some good, and we finally parted as friends.

Forty-five

Today, I woke up early at the buzz of the caretaker clearing the path up to the door of my building with his noisy snow machine. Any irritation this caused me was instantly forgotten when I remembered what day it was, and when the machine stopped I drifted back to sleep with my head full of hopeful fantasies.

Later, after showering and dressing, I watched a bit of world news on CNN before wrapping myself up and going out into the winter streets. It's a ten-minute walk from my place to the city centre, fifteen or twenty clumping through snow. I don't own a car. If I'm going any great distance there's usually a tram that will take me there, and in summer I ride a bicycle. The temperature was minus fifteen this morning but there is no wind, there rarely is here, and the snow is dry and fluffy, crunchy to walk on, and won't turn slushy until spring is around the corner.

In town, I went to my favourite café and ordered coffee and croissants. Coffee is a big thing here, the way tea is in England, and I'm afraid it puts Lily's to shame, but at least I'm fondly reminded of her every time I drink it, which is probably too often. The café is usually busy with well-heeled, well-behaved people being nice and normal. Outside, beyond the double-glazed windows, mothers leave their infants swaddled in their prams underneath the outdoor terrace heaters in the belief that the cold air is healthy for them. Maybe it is. I'm not so sure about the traffic fumes, though.

I sat there for my customary hour, reading a paperback, scribbling in my notebook, watching the world go by. It's a pleasure I still don't take for granted: not having to chase the hustle every waking hour. The freedom to enjoy simply passing the time. I don't think I've lived as contentedly as I do now since the monastery at Chiang Mai. But as I sat in the warmth of the café, I kept thinking of the risk I was about to take with my current equilibrium by inviting a new and unpredictable element into my ordered universe.

After breakfast, I loitered in the Arkadia International Bookshop for half an hour. I went to the biography section (the Finns are above having something as tacky as a 'true crime' section in their bookshops) and looked at a picture of the twelve-year-old me on the front cover of Laura Duxton's book, then at the 38-year-old me on the back cover of my own. Both books were Finnish translations and I put them back on the shelf. I went to the English-language section, stocked mainly with classic fiction, and bought a Graham Greene novel that I'd not read yet, *The Power and the Glory*. Then I walked along the avenue back to my district, where I bought dinner ingredients from the local supermarket and wine from Alko, the state-run off-licence.

Back in the flat, I spent the next hour faffing about in the kitchen, preparing a tuna lasagne that could be heated up in the oven later. Just in case it would be needed, or desirable. I didn't know. I had no plan, and no clue, as to what would unfold later. Then I started looking at my watch. Still hours to go yet and already I was feeling butterflies in my stomach.

I was too twitchy to go back to the kitchen and make myself some lunch but I knew I had to eat something so I went out to a nearby delicatessen and, for lack of imagination, bought a joyless sandwich of salt-beef and gherkin. I walked back through the local park, avoiding the areas of yellow snow where the ambassadors of various countries bring their dogs to relieve their bladders.

In the afternoon I tried to do some writing – I have a laptop and a printer now, but no wi-fi or internet – but I couldn't concentrate on it so I put on a DVD, the latest *Mission Impossible*, in the hope that it would distract me. At the end of it, I didn't know what had just happened in the last two hours, but it didn't matter. I'd killed some time.

By then, it was dark outside. I stepped out onto my second-floor balcony, where snow rose ten centimetres high on the outdoor furniture like a thick topping of meringue. I scooped some up on top of the little round table and shaped it into a snow-cone lantern, the way one of my neighbours in the block explained to me during a chat in the communal sauna. Then I went inside and fetched a tea-light and I placed it in the snow cone and lit it, then shifted the table to where the light could be seen from the street – a Finnish custom of welcome and hospitality through the long winter months.

I've reached my destination. It's time.

I take the tram back into town. I've slogged through enough snow for one day. From there I catch the Finnair City Bus for the thirty-minute ride to the airport.

The letter from Katy Stewart arrived seven weeks ago, passed on by my publishers, care of whom it had been addressed to me. It informed me that she was twice divorced, no kids, and living alone in Leicester, where she works as a librarian at the university and is worried about job security. She is now known as Kath Bradley, the latter name kept from her second marriage.

She explained that she had been approached some time ago by an author who'd just published a book about me. She didn't read any of those books and it was news to her that there was a new one out, doubly so when she heard that I had published one too. She hadn't read either of them. Normally, she would not have responded to anything media-related, she had spent most of her life shying away from all that. But the author claimed to have met me and spent time in my company.

The fact that Katy agreed to a conversation led me to read the implication between the lines that she had wanted to know where I was.

She subsequently met Laura Duxton over lunch and confirmed to her that at the time of the killing her brother was whipping her with nettles, as I had claimed but which was made little of in court, and that he had been intermittently cruel to her throughout her childhood. She refused, however, to discuss the rest of her family with Laura other than to confirm that her parents had passed away.

That first letter said little else than this. I wrote back, disclosing my home address, telling her in a nutshell what I'd been doing for the last ten years. I kept it factual, inviting no comment, until the last paragraph, where I told her how much I would like to see her, if it was something she might consider.

I didn't hear anything back for a month and I thought that was the end of it, until one snowy evening two weeks ago, when I get the phone call of my life:

'Hello, Steven? It's Kath. Kath Bradley...'

The bus arrives at the airport and I look up at the dark snow-laden sky, hoping her flight hasn't been delayed. I make my way to the arrivals hall, busy with people muffled in Gore-Tex and a few women wrapped in real fur. I check the board – it's on time – and take up my station among the mothers, fathers and children, the chauffeurs, tour organisers and taxi drivers bearing printed names on signs, and wait for her to walk through those doors.

I have a recent photo that she posted me last week so I would recognise her at the arrivals gate. No wonder I thought Laura might be her. They share the same facial shape, the same complexion, the same hair colour. In the photo, Kath's hair is shorter now. The blue eyes and high cheekbones may look the same, but only the woman in the photo possesses the unique smile that thrilled me as a boy.

My heart thumps as the passengers from the London flight begin to emerge. I check the photo again with a quick glance and look back up to see those same eyes searching for me among the crowd at the barrier. They pass me by, move back to me, lock on.

We smile at each other across the short distance and, as we both move to embrace, I imagine how nice it would be if something good and honest and true could finally come from this vile world we've both been living in.

Other books from Armley Press

In All Beginnings: Ray Brown
Whoosh!: Ray Brown
Thurso: P. James Callaghan
Stickleback: Mark Connors
Tom Tit and the Maniacs: Mark Connors
The Lost Boys of Prometheus City: A.J. Kirby
Hot Knife: John Lake
Blowback: John Lake
Speedbomb: John Lake
Amy and the Fox: John Lake
Coming Out as a Bowie Fan in Leeds, Yorkshire, England:
Mick McCann
Nailed: Mick McCann
How Leeds Changed the World: Mick McCann
Leeds, the Biography: A History of Leeds in Short Stories:
Chris Nickson
The World is (Not) a Cold Dead Place: Nathan O'Hagan
Out of the City: Nathan O'Hagan
The Last Sane Man on Earth: Nathan O'Hagan
Reliability of Rope: Samantha Priestley
A Bad Winter: Samantha Priestley
Breaking Even: David Siddall
Fogbow and Glory: K.D. Thomas
Sex & Death and Other Stories: Ivor Tymchak
20 Stories High: Michael Yates
Dying is the Last Thing You Ever Want to Do: Michael Yates

Find us at Facebook, Twitter, Amazon and armleypress.com

Lightning Source UK Ltd.
Milton Keynes UK
UKHW010959170922
408982UK00010B/286